This book belongs to

....

CLASSIC TREASURY
FAIRY TALES

Compiled by Vic Parker

Miles Kelly

First published in 2013 by Miles Kelly Publishing Ltd
Harding's Barn, Bardfield End Green, Thaxted, Essex, CM6 3PX, UK

Copyright © Miles Kelly Publishing Ltd 2013

Some of this material was first published in 2011 by
Miles Kelly Publishing Ltd as part of *50 Scary Fairy Tales*

This edition printed 2014

2 4 6 8 10 9 7 5 3

Publishing Director *Belinda Gallagher*
Creative Director *Jo Cowan*
Editorial Director *Rosie McGuire*
Senior Editor *Sarah Parkin*
Designers *Jo Cowan, Joe Jones, Venita Kidwai*
Production Manager *Elizabeth Collins*
Reprographics *Stephan Davis, Jennifer Hunt, Thom Allaway*
Assets *Lorraine King*

ISBN 978-1-78209-187-5

Printed in China

British Library Cataloguing-in-Publication Data
A catalogue record for this book is available from the British Library

ACKNOWLEDGEMENTS

The publishers would like to thank the following artists
who have contributed to this book:
Cover
Central image: Elly MacKay
Other elements: Alice Brisland at The Bright Agency, LenLis/Shutterstock.com,
kusuriuri/Shutterstock.com, Lana L/Shutterstock.com, Markovka/Shutterstock.com
Inside pages
Advocate Art: Andy Catling, Robert Dunn, Luke Finlayson
The Bright Agency: Si Clark, Peter Cottrill, Gerald Kelley, Iva Sasheva, Cherie Zamazing
Page decoration: Shutterstock.com

Made with paper from a sustainable forest

www.mileskelly.net
info@mileskelly.net

CONTENTS

WITCHES AND WARLOCKS

DARING DEEDS

MONSTERS AND MISCHIEF

TRICKS AND MISHAPS

BAD BEASTIES

ABOUT THE AUTHORS

Find information below on the authors whose stories appear in this book.

Hans Christian Andersen
1805–1875

Born in Denmark, Hans Christian Andersen was apprenticed to a weaver and a tailor, before working as an actor and singer in Copenhagen. While in the theatre he wrote poetry and stories and became famous worldwide for children's tales. These have been translated into over 150 languages, and have inspired movies, animated films, plays and ballets.

Kate Douglas Wiggin 1856–1923
Nora Archibald Smith 1859–1934

Sisters Kate and Nora were born in Philadelphia, USA. Kate started the first free kindergarten in San Francisco. Then she and Nora set up a training school for kindergarten teachers, and raised money for it by writing stories. Together, they retold and edited many collections of tales for children.

L Frank Baum
1856–1919

Lyman Frank Baum was born in New York, USA. He hated his first name and preferred to be called Frank. As a child he began writing stories, printing them on his own printing press, and later worked as a newspaper and magazine editor. Baum's greatest success was *The Wonderful Wizard of Oz*. He went on to write 13 books about the magical land of Oz, and many other short stories, poems and scripts.

Yei Theodora Ozaki
?–1933

Yei Theodora Ozaki was born into nobility, to a British mother and a Japanese father, Baron Ozaki. She married Yukio Ozaki, the Mayor of Tokyo, who was influential in international politics. Her lifelong passion was collecting and retelling ancient Japanese folk tales.

Joseph Jacobs
1854–1916

Born in Australia, Jacobs studied in England and Germany as a young man, researching Jewish history. Eventually he settled in America, and, inspired by the Brothers Grimm, went on to edit five collections of fairy tales.

Brothers Grimm
Jacob Ludwig Karl Grimm 1785–1863
Wilhelm Karl Grimm 1786–1859

Jacob and Wilhelm Grimm were born near Frankfurt, Germany. They read law at university, but were inspired to study how spoken language changes over time. This led them to collect many popular oral European folk tales and set them down on paper. Jacob did most of the research while Wilhelm did more of the writing. The brothers became librarians and also worked on compiling language books and a dictionary.

Andrew Lang
1844–1912

Scotsman Lang studied at St Andrew's
University in Fife and Balliol College, Oxford.
He researched folklore, mythology and religion,
and wrote poetry and novels. Lang adapted
12 books of folk and fairy tales for children.

Sophia Morrison
1859–1917

Born on the Isle of Man, UK, Sophia Morrison
worked there all her life to preserve its
literature, music, language and folklore.

Thomas Frederick Crane
1844–1927

American Thomas Frederick Crane worked as
a lawyer and academic, but devoted much of
his spare time to collecting folklore.

ABOUT THE ARTISTS

Andy Catling lives in Hampshire, UK. He specializes in children's illustration, but has also produced digital artwork and animation for video games. Andy likes to lend his humour and sense of character to stories with historical and fairy tale themes.
The Master and his Pupil

Si Clark graduated from Bournemouth in 2005. He moved to London, where he has been developing his illustration style and working in different fields, such as animation and design.
The Prince and the Dragon • The Devil and his Grandmother
The Jelly Fish and the Monkey

Peter Cottrill enjoys creating stories and scenarios. Humour and a sense of the absurd inspire him. For Peter, a brief is a chance to be creative and see what he can come up with, whatever the subject. Peter also does some teaching and practises Shiatsu.
Aladdin and the Wonderful Lamp • The Wicked Witch of the West
The Dragon of the North • The History of Jack the Giant-Killer • Tom Tit Tot
Mr Miacca • The Singing Bone • Schippeitaro

Robert Dunn studied Fine Art at college. He creates images with watercolour and pencil, and then adds the finishing touches digitally. Robert has worked on classic fiction collections, picture books and magazines.
The Buggane of the Church

Luke Finlayson enrolled at a 2D animation school and studied for three years, before working on various animated shows. He later turned to illustration. Luke has a great love of stories of wild imagination, and he is inspired by fairy tales.
The King who would see Paradise • Beauty and the Beast

About the Artists

Gerald Kelley works from his studio in Denver, Colorado, USA. He began working in watercolour and pencil, but now works digitally, from sketch to finished artwork. Illustrators Arthur Rackham and Edmund Dulac are major inspirations in Gerald's work. He loves illustrating fantastical and scary stories.

The Witch • The Horned Women • Rapunzel • Hansel and Grettel • Rushen Coatie
The Demon with the Matted Hair • The Third Voyage of Sinbad the Sailor • Buchettino
The Twelve Brothers • The Story of the Fisherman • The Ogre of Rashomon
The Red Shoes • The Ratcatcher • The Farmer and the Badger • The Strange Visitor

Elly MacKay is a graduate of the Nova Scotia College of Art and Design, where she studied illustration, printmaking and electronic art. Her work has been shown in Canadian galleries and is sold in several stores. Elly lives in Owen Sound, Ontario, Canada with her husband and daughter.

Cover

Iva Sasheva lives in Los Angeles. She took her Master in Fine Graphic Arts. Iva has collaborated with authors in the creation of graphic novels and children's books. She also works as a storyboard artist for feature films and commercials. Iva writes short stories, which she illustrates as well.

The Little Mermaid • Jorinda and Jorindel • Tamlane • The Goblin Pony

Cherie Zamazing graduated from Loughborough University in 2005, completing a degree in Illustration. She likes to work in a variety of styles, keeping her work fresh and adapting it to suit a variety of age groups. Cherie has recently started to create her own stories and has thoroughly enjoyed illustrating them, giving her imagination a real work out.

The Mandarin and the Butterfly • The Snow Queen • Little Red Riding Hood

WITCHES AND WÄRLOCKS

The Witch

A Russian fairy tale, based on the Baba Yaga folk story,
from Andrew Lang's *Yellow Fairy Book*

Once upon a time there was a peasant whose wife died, leaving him with twins. For some years the poor man cared for the children, but at last he married again. However, the twins' new stepmother was cruel to them. All day she thought of nothing but how she could get rid of them.

At last an evil idea came to her, and one morning she said, "I am going to send you to visit my granny, who lives in a dear little hut in the wood. You will have to work hard for her, but she will take good care of you."

So the children left the house and entered the great gloomy wood, with only a bottle of milk, a piece of ham and a hunk of bread. The little sister, who was very wise for her years, said to the brother, "Our stepmother is not sending us to her granny, but to a wicked witch. We must be polite and kind to everyone, and never touch a crumb belonging to anyone else. Then someone might help us."

Eventually, the children saw in the thickest of the trees a little hut. Nervously they peeped inside – and there lay the witch, with her head on the threshold, a foot in each corner and her knees pushed up, almost touching the ceiling. "Who's there?" she snarled.

Though the twins were terrified, they answered politely. "Good morning, Granny. Our stepmother has sent us to serve you."

"See that you do it well, then," growled the witch. "If I am pleased with you, I'll reward you, but if I am not, I'll cook you in the oven!"

So saying, she set the girl down to spin yarn, and she gave the boy a sieve in which to carry water from the well, and she herself went out into the wood.

The girl began weeping bitterly because she could not spin. But suddenly she heard hundreds of little feet, and from every hole in the hut mice came pattering, squeaking and saying,

"Little girl, why are your eyes so red?

If you want help, then give us some bread."

And the girl gave them some of her bread. Then the mice told her that the witch had a cat, and the cat was very fond of ham. If she would give the cat her ham, it would show her the way out of the wood, and in the meantime they would spin the yarn for her. So the girl set out to look for the cat and, as she was hunting about, she met her brother. He was in great trouble because he could not carry water from the well in a sieve, as it came pouring out as fast as he put it in.

As she was trying to comfort him they heard a rustling of wings, and a flight of wrens alighted on the ground beside them. The wrens said,

"Give us some crumbs, then you need not grieve.

For you'll find that water will stay in the sieve."

Then the twins crumbled some of their bread on the ground, and the wrens pecked it and chirped. When they had eaten the last crumb they told the boy to fill up the holes of the sieve with clay, and then to draw water from the well. So he did what they said, and carried the sieve full of water into the hut without spilling a drop.

When they entered the hut the cat was curled up on the floor. They stroked her and fed her with ham, and then said to her, "Puss, tell us how to get away from the witch."

The cat thanked them for the ham, and gave

them a pocket-handkerchief and a comb. Then the cat told the children what they should do with them to escape. The cat had scarcely finished speaking when the witch returned.

"Well, you have done well enough for today," she grumbled, "but tomorrow you'll have something more difficult to do, and if you don't do it well, straight into the oven you will go."

The poor children were very frightened, and they lay down to sleep on a heap of straw in the corner of the hut. But they dared not close their eyes and scarcely breathed.

In the morning the witch gave the girl two pieces of linen to weave before night, and the boy a pile of wood to chop. Then the witch left them to their tasks and went out into the wood.

As soon as she was out of sight the children took the comb and the handkerchief and, holding hands, they ran, and ran, and ran. First they met the witch's watchdog, who was going to chase them, but they threw the remains of their bread to him, and he ate it and wagged his tail. Then they were hindered by the birch trees, whose branches almost scratched them. But the little sister tied the twigs together with her hair ribbon, and they got past safely and came out onto the open fields.

In the meantime, in the hut, the cat was busy weaving the linen. The witch returned to see how the children were getting on. She crept up to the window and said, "Are you weaving, my dear?"

"Yes, Granny, I am weaving," answered the cat.

Then the witch realized that the children had escaped! She was furious and shouted at the cat, "Why did you let the children leave the hut?"

But the cat spat and answered, "I have served you all these years and you never even threw me a bone, but the children gave me their own piece of ham."

Then the witch was furious with the watchdog and birch trees, because they had let the children pass. But the dog said, "I have served you all these years and you never gave me so much as a crust, but the children gave me their own loaf of bread."

And the birch rustled its leaves and said, "I have served you longer than I can say, and you never even tied a bit of twine round my branches, but the children bound them up with their bright ribbon."

So the witch saw there was no help to be got from her old servants, and she mounted her broom and set off after the children herself. As the twins ran they heard the sound of the broom close behind them. They remembered what the cat had told them and threw the handkerchief over their shoulders. Instantly, a deep, broad river flowed behind them.

It took the witch a long time to find a place to ride over on her broomstick, but at last she got across, and continued the chase faster than before.

As the children ran they heard the broom close behind them. So, quick as thought, they did what the cat had told them and threw the comb on the ground. In an instant, a dense forest sprang up, in which the roots and branches were so closely intertwined, that it was impossible to force a way through it. When the witch came to it she found

that there was nothing for it but to turn round and go back to her hut, tearing her hair with rage.

The twins ran straight on till they reached their home. They told their father all that they had suffered, and he was so angry with their stepmother that he drove her out of the house and never let her return. Then the children and their father lived happily ever after.

Aladdin and the Wonderful Lamp

An extract from *The Arabian Nights Entertainments*,
retold by Andrew Lang

There once lived a poor tailor, who had a son called Aladdin – a careless, idle boy who would do nothing but play all day long in the streets with other idle boys like himself. This so grieved the father that he died. Yet, in spite of his mother's tears and prayers, Aladdin did not mend his ways. One day, when he was playing in the streets as usual, a stranger asked him his age and if he was the son of Mustapha the tailor.

"I am, sir," replied Aladdin, "but he died a long while ago."

On this the stranger, who was a famous African magician, hugged him and kissed him, saying, "I am your uncle! I recognized you because you look so like my brother. You must go to your mother and tell her I am coming."

Aladdin ran home and told his mother of his newly found uncle.

"Indeed, child," she said, "your father had a brother, but I always thought he was dead."

However, she prepared supper and told Aladdin to get ready to welcome his uncle.

The strange man came laden with gifts of wine and fruit. He kissed the place where Mustapha used to sit, bidding Aladdin's mother not to be surprised at not having seen him before, as he had been out of the country for forty years. He then turned to Aladdin and asked him his trade, at which the boy hung his head, while his mother burst into tears. On learning that Aladdin was idle and refused to learn a trade, he offered to rent a shop and stock it for him. The very next day he bought Aladdin a fine suit of clothes and took him all over the city, showing him the sights. At nightfall, he brought Aladdin home to his mother, who was overjoyed to see her son so fine.

On the following day, he led Aladdin into some beautiful gardens a long way outside the city gates. They sat down by a fountain and the magician pulled a cake from his girdle, which he divided between them. Then they journeyed onwards till they almost reached the mountains. Aladdin was so tired that he begged to go back, but the magician won him over with pleasant stories and led him on.

At last they came to two mountains divided by a narrow valley.

"We will go no farther," said the magician. "I will show you something wonderful. You gather up sticks while I kindle a fire."

When the fire was lit the magician threw a powder on it, at the same time as saying some magical words. The earth trembled a little and opened in front of them to show a square, flat stone with a brass ring in the middle to raise it by.

Aladdin tried to run away, but the magician caught him and gave him a blow that knocked him down.

"What have I done, Uncle?" Aladdin begged.

The magician replied, more kindly, "Fear nothing, but obey me. Beneath this stone lies a treasure that is to be yours, and no one else may touch it, so you must do exactly as I tell you."

At the word 'treasure', Aladdin forgot his fears and grasped the ring as he was told, saying the names of his father and grandfather. The stone came up quite easily and some steps appeared.

"Go down," said the magician. "At the foot of those steps you will find an open door leading into three large halls. Tuck up your gown and go through them without touching anything, or you will die instantly. These halls lead into a garden of fine fruit trees. Walk on till you come to an alcove in a terrace, where stands a lighted lamp. Pour out the oil it contains and bring the lamp to me."

The magician drew a ring from his finger and gave it to Aladdin, wishing him good luck.

Nervously, Aladdin crept down the stairs. He found everything as the magician had said. Aladdin gathered some fruit off the trees, got the lamp, and hurried back to the mouth of the cave.

The magician cried out, "Make haste and give me the lamp."

But Aladdin was suspicious. "Only when I'm safely out of the cave," he yelled back.

The magician flew into a terrible rage. Throwing some more powder on the fire, he said more magic words, and the stone rolled back into its place.

The magician left Persia forever, which plainly showed that he was no uncle of Aladdin's. He was a cunning magician who had read in his magic books of a wonderful lamp, which would make him the most powerful man in the world. Though he alone knew where to find it, he could only receive it from the hand of another. He had picked out the foolish Aladdin for this purpose, intending to get the lamp and then kill him.

For two days Aladdin remained in the dark, crying and wailing. At last he clasped his hands in prayer, and in doing so rubbed the ring, which the magician had forgotten to take from him. Immediately an enormous and frightful genie rose out of it, saying, "What do you want from me? I am the Slave of the Ring and will obey you in all things."

Aladdin fearlessly replied, "Deliver me from this place!" Whereupon the earth opened and he found himself outside. As soon as his eyes could bear the light he went home, where he fainted from exhaustion and shock the minute he walked through the door.

When he came to, Aladdin told his mother what had happened, and showed her the lamp and the fruits he had gathered in the garden, which were in reality precious stones. He then asked for some food.

"Alas, child!" she said. "Our

cupboards are bare. But I have spun a little cotton, and will go and sell it."

"No," Aladdin protested. "You keep the cotton. I'll go and sell this rusty old lamp instead."

The lamp was indeed very dirty, and Aladdin's mother began to rub it to clean it, so that it might fetch a higher price. Instantly a hideous genie appeared and asked what she wanted. She fainted, but Aladdin, snatching the lamp, said boldly, "Fetch us something to eat!"

The genie returned with a silver bowl, twelve silver plates containing rich meats, two silver cups and two bottles of wine.

Aladdin's mother came to and couldn't believe her eyes. "Wherever did all this come from?" she said.

"Don't ask, just eat," Aladdin replied, grinning.

So they sat and tucked in, and Aladdin told his mother about the lamp. She begged him to sell it and have nothing to do with devils.

"No," said Aladdin, "luck has brought it to me, so

we will use it – and the ring too."

When they had eaten everything the genie had brought, Aladdin sold the silver plates. He then summoned the genie, who gave him another set of plates – and thus they lived for many years.

The Little Mermaid

An extract from the tale by Hans Christian Andersen

The little mermaid went out from her garden and took the road to the foaming whirlpools, behind which the sorceress lived. She had never been that way before. Neither flowers nor grass grew there. Nothing but bare, grey, sandy ground stretched out to the whirlpools, where the water, like foaming mill-wheels, whirled round everything that it seized, and cast it into the fathomless deep.

Through the midst of these crushing whirlpools the little mermaid was obliged to pass, to reach the dominions of the sea witch. Also, for a long distance, the only road lay right across a quantity of warm, bubbling mire, called by the witch her turfmoor. Beyond this stood her house, in the centre of a strange forest, in which all the trees and flowers were polypi, half animals and half plants. They looked like serpents with a hundred heads growing out of the ground. The branches were long slimy arms, with fingers like flexible worms, moving limb after limb from the root to the top. All that could be reached in the sea they seized and held fast, so that it never escaped from their clutches.

The little mermaid was so alarmed at what she saw that she stood still, and her heart beat with fear, and she was very nearly turned back. But she thought of the prince, and of the human soul for which she longed, and her courage returned. She fastened her long, flowing hair round her head, so that the polypi might not seize hold of it. Then she darted forwards as a fish shoots through the water, between the supple arms and fingers of the ugly polypi, which were stretched out on each side of her. She saw that each held in its grasp something it had seized with its numerous little arms, as if they were iron bands. The white skeletons of human beings who had perished at sea, and had sunk down into the deep waters, skeletons of land animals, oars, rudders and chests of ships were lying tightly grasped by their clinging arms.

She now came to a space of marshy ground in the wood, where large, fat water-snakes were rolling in the mire and showing their ugly, drab-coloured bodies. In the midst of this spot stood a house, built with the bones of shipwrecked human beings. There sat the sea witch, allowing a toad to eat from her mouth. She called the ugly water-snakes her little chickens, and allowed them to crawl all over her.

"I know what you want," said the sea witch. "It is very stupid of you, but you shall have your way, and it will bring you to sorrow, my pretty princess. You want to get rid of your fish's tail, and to have two supports instead of it, like human beings on earth, so that the young prince may fall in love with you,

and that you may have an immortal soul." And then the witch laughed so loud and disgustingly that the toad and the snakes fell to the ground and lay there wriggling about.

"You are just in time," said the witch, "for after sunrise tomorrow I should not be able to help you till the end of another year. I will prepare a magic potion for you, with which you must swim to land tomorrow before sunrise, and sit down on the shore and drink it. Your tail will then disappear, and shrink up into what mankind calls legs. You will feel great pain, as if a sword were passing through you. But all who see you will say that you are the prettiest little human being they ever saw. You will still have the same floating gracefulness of movement, and no dancer will ever tread so lightly. But at every step you take it will feel as if you were treading upon sharp knives. If you will bear all this, I will help you."

"Yes, I will," said the princess in a trembling voice, thinking of the prince and the immortal soul.

"But think again," said the witch, "for once your shape has become like a human being, you can no longer be a mermaid. You will never return through the water to your sisters, or to your father's palace again. And if you do not win the love of the prince, so that he is willing to forget his father and mother for your sake, and to love you with his whole soul, and to allow the priest to join your hands that you may be man and wife, then you will never have an immortal soul. The first morning after he marries another your heart will break, and you will become foam on the crest of the waves."

"I will do it," said the little mermaid, and she became pale as death.

"But I must be paid also," said the witch, "and it is not a trifle that I ask. You have the sweetest voice of any who dwell here in the depths of the sea, and you believe that you will be able to charm the prince with it also, but this voice you must give to me. The best thing you possess will I have for the price of my draught. My own blood must be mixed with it, that it may be as sharp as a two-edged sword."

"But if you take away my voice," said the little mermaid, "what is left for me?"

"Your beautiful form, your graceful walk and your expressive eyes – surely with these you can enchain a man's heart? Well, have you lost your courage? Put out your little tongue that I may cut it off as my payment, and then you shall have the powerful draught."

"It shall be," said the little mermaid.

Then the witch placed her cauldron on the fire to prepare the magic potion.

"Cleanliness is a good thing," said she, scouring the vessel with snakes, which she had tied together in a large knot. Then she pricked herself in the breast, and let the black blood drop into it. The steam that rose formed itself into such horrible shapes that no one could look at them without fear. Every moment the witch threw something else into the vessel, and when it began to boil, the sound was like the weeping of a crocodile. When at last the

magic potion was ready, it looked like the clearest water. "There it is for you," said the witch. Then she cut off the mermaid's tongue, so that she became dumb, and would never again speak or sing.

"If the polypi should seize hold of you as you return through the wood," said the witch, "throw over them a few drops of the potion, and their fingers will be torn into a thousand pieces." But the little mermaid had no occasion to do this, for the polypi sprang back in terror when they caught sight of the glittering potion, which shone in her hand like a twinkling star.

So she passed quickly through the wood and the marsh, and between the rushing whirlpools. She saw that in her father's palace the torches in the ballroom were extinguished, and all within asleep. But she did not venture to go in to them, for now she was dumb and going to leave them forever, she felt as if her heart would break. The little mermaid stole into the garden, took a flower from the flowerbeds of each of her sisters, kissed her hand a thousand times towards the palace, and then rose up through the dark blue waters.

The Wicked Witch of the West

Adapted from *The Wonderful Wizard of Oz*
by L Frank Baum

*Dorothy and her little dog Toto are in the Land of Oz. The Good Witch
of the North gives her some silver shoes, and tells her that to return home
she must go to the Emerald City and ask the Wizard of Oz for help.
Dorothy travels down the Yellow Brick Road, befriending the Scarecrow,
the Tin Woodman and the Cowardly Lion, who go with her. When they
finally reach the Wizard, he agrees to help them – but only if they can
kill the Wicked Witch of the West, who rules over the Winkie Country.*

The soldier with the green whiskers led them
to the gate out of the Emerald City.

"Which road leads to the Wicked Witch of the
West?" asked Dorothy.

"There is no road," answered the Guardian of the

Gates. "No one ever wishes to go that way."

"How, then, are we to find her?" enquired the girl.

"That will be easy," replied the Guardian of the Gates, "walk to the West, and when she knows you are in the country of the Winkies, she will find you and make you all her slaves."

"Perhaps not," said the Scarecrow, "for we mean to destroy her."

So they turned toward the West, walking over fields of soft grass dotted here and there with daisies and buttercups. The Emerald City was soon left far behind. And as they advanced the ground became rougher and hillier, for there were no farms nor houses in this country of the West, and the ground was untilled.

In the afternoon the sun shone hot in their faces, for there were no trees to offer them shade. So, Dorothy and Toto and the Lion were tired, and lay down upon the grass and fell asleep, with the Woodman and the Scarecrow keeping watch.

Now the Wicked Witch of the West had but one eye, yet that was as powerful as a telescope, and could see everywhere. So, as she sat in the door of her castle, she happened to look around and saw Dorothy lying asleep, with her friends all about her. They were a long distance off, but the Wicked Witch was angry to find them in her country. So she blew upon a silver whistle that hung around her neck.

At once there came running to her from all directions a pack of great wolves. They had long legs and fierce eyes and sharp teeth.

"Go to those people," said the Witch, "and tear them to pieces."

"Are you not going to make them your slaves?" asked the leader of the wolves.

"No," the Witch answered, "one is of tin, and one of straw, one is a girl and another a lion. None of them is fit to work, so you may tear them all into small pieces."

"Very well," said the wolf, and he dashed away at

full speed, followed by the others.

It was lucky the Scarecrow and the Woodman were wide awake and heard the wolves coming.

"This is my fight," said the Woodman, "so get behind me and I will meet them as they come."

He seized his axe, which he had made very sharp, and as the leader of the wolves came on, the Tin Woodman swung his arm and chopped the wolf's head from its body, so that it immediately died. As soon as he could raise his axe another wolf came up, and he also fell under the sharp edge of the Tin Woodman's weapon. There were forty wolves, and forty times a

wolf was killed, so that at last they all lay dead in a heap before the Woodman.

Then he put down his axe and sat beside the Scarecrow, who said, "It was a good fight, friend."

They waited until Dorothy awoke the next morning. The little girl was quite frightened when she saw the great pile of shaggy wolves, but the Tin Woodman told her all. She thanked him for saving them and sat down to breakfast, after which they started again upon their journey.

Now this same morning the Wicked Witch came to the door of her castle and looked out with her one eye that could see far off. She saw all of her wolves lying dead, and the strangers still travelling through her country. This made her even angrier than before, and she blew her silver whistle twice.

A great flock of wild crows

came flying toward her, enough to darken the sky.

And the Wicked Witch said to the King Crow, "Fly to the strangers. Peck out their eyes and tear them to pieces."

The wild crows flew in one great flock toward Dorothy and her companions. When the little girl saw them coming she was afraid.

But the Scarecrow said, "This is my battle, so lie down beside me and you will not be harmed."

So they all lay upon the ground except the Scarecrow, who stood up and stretched out his arms. And when the flock of wild crows saw him they were frightened, as these birds always are by scarecrows, and did not dare to come any nearer. But the King Crow said, "It is only a stuffed man. I will peck his eyes out."

The King Crow flew at the Scarecrow, who caught it by the head and twisted its neck until it died. And then another crow flew at him, and the Scarecrow twisted its neck also. Soon there were forty crows, and forty times the Scarecrow twisted a neck, until at last all were lying dead beside him. Then he called to his companions to rise, and again they started upon their journey.

When the Wicked Witch looked out again and saw all her crows lying in a heap, she got into a terrible rage, and blew three times upon her silver whistle.

Forthwith there was heard a great buzzing in the air, and a swarm of black bees came flying toward her.

"Go to the strangers and sting them to death!" commanded the Witch, and the bees turned and flew rapidly until they came to where

Dorothy and her friends were walking. But the Woodman had seen them coming, and the Scarecrow had decided what to do.

"Take out my straw and scatter it over the little girl and the dog and the Lion," he said to the Woodman. "Then the bees will not be able to sting them." This the Woodman did, and as Dorothy lay close beside the Lion and held Toto in her arms, the straw covered them entirely. The bees came and found no one but the Woodman to sting, so they flew at him and broke off all their stings against the tin, without hurting the Woodman at all. And as bees cannot live when their stings are broken, that was the end of them, and they lay scattered thick about the Woodman, like little heaps of fine coal.

Then Dorothy and the Lion got up, and the girl helped the Tin Woodman put the straw back into the Scarecrow again, until he was as good as ever. So they started upon their journey once more.

The Wicked Witch was so angry when she saw her black bees in little heaps like fine coal that she stamped her foot and tore her hair and gnashed her teeth. And then she called a dozen of her slaves, who were the Winkies, and gave them sharp spears, telling them to go to the strangers and destroy them.

The Winkies were not a brave people, but they had to do as they were told. So they marched away until they came near to Dorothy. Then the Lion gave a great roar and sprang towards them, and the poor Winkies were so frightened that they ran back as fast as they could.

When they returned to the castle the Wicked

Witch was very cross and sent them back to their work, after which she sat down to think what she should do next. She could not understand how all her plans to destroy these strangers had failed. But she was a powerful witch, as well as a wicked one, and she soon made up her mind how to act.

There was, in her cupboard, a Golden Cap, with a circle of diamonds and rubies running round it. This Golden Cap had a charm. Whoever owned it could call three times upon the Winged Monkeys, who would obey any order they were given. But no person could command these strange creatures more than three times.

Twice already the Wicked Witch had used the charm of the Cap. Once was when she had made the Winkies her slaves, and set herself to rule over their country. The Winged Monkeys had helped her do this. The second time was when she had fought against the Great Oz himself, and driven him out of the land of the West. The Winged Monkeys had also helped her in doing this.

Only once more could the Wicked Witch use this Golden Cap, for which reason she did not like to do so until all her other powers were exhausted. But now that her wolves and her crows and her bees were gone, and her slaves had been scared away by the Cowardly Lion, she saw there was only one way left to destroy Dorothy and her friends.

So the Wicked Witch took the Golden Cap and placed it on her head. Then she stood upon her left foot and said slowly, "Ep-pe, pep-pe, kak-ke!"

Next she stood upon her right foot and said, "Hil-lo, hol-lo, hel-lo!"

After this she stood upon both feet and cried in a loud voice, "Ziz-zy, zuz-zy, zik!"

The charm began to work. The sky darkened and a rumbling sound was heard. There was a rushing of wings, a chattering and laughing, and the sun came out to show the Wicked Witch surrounded by monkeys, each with a pair of wings on his shoulders.

One, the leader, and bigger than the others, flew

down to the Witch and said, "You have called us for the third and last time. What do you command?"

"Go to the strangers who are within my land and destroy them all except the Lion," said the Wicked Witch. "Bring that beast to me, for I have a mind to harness him like a horse and make him work."

"Your commands shall be obeyed," said the big monkey. Then, with a great deal of chattering and noise, the huge crowd of Winged Monkeys flew away to find the place where Dorothy and her three friends were walking.

Some of the monkeys seized the Tin Woodman and carried him through the air until they were over a country that was thickly covered with sharp rocks. Here they dropped the poor Woodman, who fell a great distance to the rocks, where he lay so battered and dented that he could neither move nor groan.

Some other monkeys caught the Scarecrow, and with their long fingers pulled all of the straw out of his clothes and head. They made his hat and boots and clothes into a small bundle and threw it into

the top branches of a tall tree.

The remaining monkeys threw pieces of stout rope around the Lion and wound many coils about his body and head and legs, until he was unable to bite or scratch or struggle in any way. Then the monkeys lifted him up and flew away with him to the Witch's castle, where he was placed in a small yard with a high iron fence around it, so that he could not escape.

But Dorothy they did not harm at all. She stood, with Toto in her arms, watching the awful fate of all her comrades and thinking it would soon be her turn. The leader of the Winged Monkeys flew up to her, his long, hairy arms stretched out and his ugly, cruel face grinning terribly, but then he saw the mark of the Good Witch's kiss upon Dorothy's forehead and stopped at once, motioning the other monkeys not to touch her.

"We cannot harm this little girl," he ordered them, "for look, she has the protection of the Power of Good, and that is far, far greater than the Power of Evil. The very most we can do is to transport her with care to the castle of the Wicked Witch and leave her there."

So, carefully and gently, they lifted Dorothy in their arms and carried her swiftly through the air until they came to the castle, where they set her down upon the front doorstep. Then the leader said to the Witch, "We have obeyed you as far as we were able. Your power over our band is now ended, and you will never see us again." Then all the Winged Monkeys, with much laughing and chattering and noise, flew into the air and were soon out of sight.

The Wicked Witch looked down at Dorothy's feet, and seeing the Silver Shoes, began to tremble with fear, for she knew what a powerful charm belonged to them. But then she looked into the child's eyes and saw that the little girl did not know of the wonderful power the Silver Shoes gave her. So the Wicked Witch laughed to herself, and said to Dorothy, very harshly and severely, "Come with me little girl, and see that you listen carefully to everything I tell you, for if you do not I will surely make an end of you, as I did of the Tin Woodman and the Scarecrow."

So Dorothy became a slave for the Wicked Witch, and realized that it would be harder than ever to get back to Kansas again.

The Horned Women

From Joseph Jacobs' *Celtic Fairy Tales*

A rich woman sat up late one night carding wool, while all the family and servants were asleep. Suddenly there came a loud knock at the door and a voice outside called, "Open! Open!"

"Who is there?" said the woman of the house.

"I am the Witch of one Horn," came the answer.

The mistress opened the door and a woman with a horn growing on her forehead entered, holding a pair of wool carders. She sat down by the fire in silence, and began to card the wool with violent haste. Suddenly she paused, and said aloud, "Where are the women? They delay too long."

Then a second knock came to the door, and a voice called, "Open! Open!"

The mistress felt herself obliged to rise and open the door, and immediately a second witch entered, having two horns on her forehead, and in her hand a wheel for spinning wool.

"Give me a place," she said. "I am the Witch of two Horns," and she began to spin quickly.

And so the knocks went on, and the call was heard, and the witches entered, until at last twelve women sat round the fire – the first with one horn, the last with twelve horns. And they carded the thread, and turned their spinning wheels, and wound and wove, all singing together an ancient rhyme, but they didn't speak a word to the mistress of the house. Strange to hear and frightful to look upon were these twelve women, with their horns and their wheels. The mistress was frightened to death and tried to get up to call for help, but she could not move, nor could she utter a word or a cry, for the spell of the witches was upon her.

Then one of them called to her, "Rise and make us a cake."

Then the mistress searched for a jug to bring water from the well that she might make the cake mix, but she couldn't find one.

And the witches said to her, "Take a sieve and bring water in it."

So she took the sieve and went to the well. But the water poured through the holes, and she sat down by the well and wept.

Then a voice from the well said, "Take yellow

clay and moss, and bind them together, and plaster the sieve so that it will hold."

This she did, and the sieve held the water.

Then the voice said again, "Go back to the house, and just before you enter, cry aloud three times, 'The mountain and the sky over it is all on fire.'"

And she did so.

When the witches inside heard the call, a great and terrible cry broke from their lips. They rushed forth with wild shrieks, and fled away back home.

Then the Spirit of the Well told the mistress of the house to enter and prepare her home against the enchantments of the witches if they returned again.

First, to break their spells, she sprinkled the water in which she had washed her child's feet, outside the door. Secondly, she took the cake, which in her absence the witches had made of meal mixed with blood drawn from her sleeping family, and she broke it in bits. Then she placed a bit in the mouth of each sleeper, and they woke up, free from the witches' power. Lastly, she secured the door with a great crossbeam barred against it, so that the witches could not enter.

The witches weren't long in coming back, and they raged and called for vengeance.

"Open! Open, feet-water!" they screamed.

"I cannot," said the feet-water. "I am scattered on the ground, trickling away to the lake."

"Open! Open, wood and trees and beam!" they cried to the door.

"I cannot," said the door, "for I am fixed and have no power to move."

"Open! Open, cake that we have made and mingled with blood!" they cried again.

"I cannot," said the cake, "for I am completely broken and bruised."

Then the witches fled back home, uttering strange curses on the Spirit of the Well. And the mistress and the house were left in peace.

The Master and his Pupil

Based on the folk tale of the sorcerer's apprentice,
retold by Joseph Jacobs in *English Fairy Tales*

There was once a very learned man in the north-country who knew all the languages under the sun, and who was acquainted with all the mysteries of creation. He had one big book bound in black leather and clasped with iron, and chained to a table that was made fast to the floor. When he read out of this book, he unlocked it with an iron key, and none but he read from it, for it contained all the secrets of the spirit world. It told how many angels there were in heaven, and how they marched in their ranks, and sang in their choirs, and what their names and jobs were. And it told of the demons, how many there were, and what their names and powers were, and how they might be summoned, and made to do people's bidding.

Now the master had a pupil who was but a foolish lad. He acted as a servant, and was never allowed to look into the black book, or hardly to enter the private room.

One day the master was out, and the lad, as curious as could be, hurried to the magical chamber. He gazed at his master's wondrous apparatus for changing copper into gold and lead into silver, and the mirror in which his master could see all that was passing in the world, and the shell that whispered to his master what people were saying at that very moment. But the lad realized he could do nothing with these things. "I don't know the right words to utter," he sighed. "They are locked up in the big black book."

He looked round and saw that the book was unfastened! The master had forgotten to lock it!

The boy rushed to it and opened the volume. It was written with red-and-black ink, and much of it he could not understand. But he put his finger on a line and spelled it through.

At once the room was darkened and the house trembled. A clap of thunder rolled through the passage and the old room, and there stood before him a horrible, horrible form, breathing fire, and with eyes like burning lamps. It was the demon Beelzebub, whom he had called up to serve him.

"Set me a task!" bellowed Beelzebub, with a voice like the roaring of an iron furnace.

The boy only trembled, and his hair stood up.

"Set me a task, or I shall strangle thee!"

But the lad could not speak.

Then the evil spirit stepped towards him, and putting forth his hands, touched his throat. The fingers burned his flesh. "Set me a task!"

"Water that flower over there," cried the boy in despair, pointing to a geranium that stood in a pot on the floor.

Instantly the spirit left the room, but in another instant he returned with a barrel on his back, and poured its contents over the flower. And again and again he went and came, and poured more and more water, till it was ankle-deep on the floor of the room.

"Enough, enough!" gasped the lad, but the demon heeded him not. The lad didn't know the words by which to send him away, and still he fetched water.

It rose to the boy's knees and still more water was poured. It mounted to his waist, and Beelzebub still kept on bringing barrels full. It rose to his armpits, and he scrambled to the tabletop. And now the water in the room stood up to the window and washed against the glass, and swirled around his feet on the table. It still rose – it reached his breast. In vain he cried – the evil spirit would not be dismissed, and to this day he would have been pouring water, and would have drowned all the world. But the master remembered on his journey that he had not locked his book, and therefore returned. At the moment when the water was bubbling about the pupil's chin, he rushed into the room and spoke the words that cast Beelzebub back into his fiery home.

Rapunzel

Retold by Andrew Lang in his *Red Fairy Book*,
after the Brothers Grimm

Once upon a time there lived a man and his
wife who were very unhappy because they had
no children. These good people had a little window
at the back of their house, which looked into the
most lovely garden. But the garden was surrounded
by a high wall, and no one dared to enter it, for it
belonged to a witch of great power, who was feared
by the whole world.

One day the woman stood at the window
overlooking the garden, and saw there a bed full of
the finest rampion – the leaves looked so fresh and

green that she longed to eat them. The desire grew day by day, and just because she knew she couldn't possibly get any, she pined away and became quite pale and wretched. Then her husband grew alarmed and said, "What ails you, dear wife?"

"Oh," she answered, "if I don't get some of that rampion to eat I know I shall die."

The man, who loved her dearly, thought to himself, 'Rather than let my wife die I will fetch her some rampion, no matter the cost.' So at dusk he climbed over the wall into the witch's garden and, hastily gathering a handful of rampion leaves, he

returned with them to his wife. She made them into a salad, which tasted so good that her longing for the forbidden food was greater than ever. If she were to know any peace of mind, there was nothing for it but that her husband should climb over the garden wall again, and fetch her some more.

So at dusk he went over the wall, but when he reached the other side he drew back in terror, for there, standing before him, was the old witch.

"How dare you," she shrieked, "climb into my garden and steal my rampion like a common thief? You shall suffer for your foolhardiness."

"Oh!" he implored. "Forgive me but I was desperate. My wife saw your rampion from her window and longs for some so badly that she will surely die if she does not have some."

Then the witch grew calmer and said, "If it's as you say, you may take as much rampion as you like, but on one condition only – that you give me the child your wife will shortly bring into the world."

The man in his terror agreed. So as soon as the

child was born the witch appeared, and having given it the name of Rapunzel, which is the same as rampion, she carried it off.

Rapunzel was the most beautiful child under the sun. When she was twelve years old, the witch shut her up in a tower in the middle of a great wood. The tower had neither stairs nor doors, only a small window high up at the very top. When the old witch wanted to get in she stood underneath and called out,

"Rapunzel, Rapunzel,
Let down your golden hair,"

for Rapunzel had wonderful long hair, and it was as fine as spun gold. Whenever she heard the witch's voice she unloosed her plaits, and let her hair fall down out of the window about twenty metres below, and the old witch climbed up by it.

After they had lived like this for a few years, it happened one day that a prince was riding through the wood and passed by the tower. As he drew near it he heard someone singing so sweetly that he stood still and listened. It was lonely Rapunzel trying to while away the time by letting her sweet voice ring out into the wood. The prince longed to see the owner of the voice, but he sought in vain for a door in the tower. He rode home, but he was so haunted by the song he had heard that he returned every day to the wood and listened. One day, when he was standing behind a tree, he saw the old witch approach and heard her call out,

"Rapunzel, Rapunzel,
  Let down your golden hair,"

then Rapunzel let down her plaits, and the witch climbed up by them.

"So that's the staircase, is it?" said the prince. "Then I too will climb it and try my luck."

So on the following day, at dusk, he went to the foot of the tower and cried,

"Rapunzel, Rapunzel,
  Let down your golden hair,"

and as soon as she had let it down the prince climbed up by it.

At first Rapunzel was terribly frightened when a man came in, but the prince spoke to her so kindly that very soon Rapunzel forgot her fear. When he asked her to marry him she consented at once. For, she thought, 'He is young and handsome, and I'll certainly be happier with him than with the old witch.' So she put her hand in his and said, "Yes, I will gladly go with you, only how am I to get down out of the tower? Every time you come to see me you must bring a skein of silk with you, and I will make a ladder of them, and when it is finished I will climb down by it, and you will take me away with you on your horse."

They arranged that till the ladder was ready, he was to come to her every evening, because the witch was with her during the day. The old witch, of course, knew nothing of what was going on, till one day Rapunzel, not thinking of what she was about, turned to her and said, "How is it, good mother, that you are so much harder to pull up than the young prince? He is always with me in a moment."

"Oh, you wicked child!" cried the witch. "I thought I had hidden you safely from the whole world but you have deceived me."

In her wrath she seized Rapunzel's beautiful hair and a pair of scissors – snip snap, off it came, and the beautiful plaits lay on the ground. And, worse than this, she was so hard-hearted that she took Rapunzel to a desert place, and there left her to live in loneliness and misery.

That same evening, the witch fastened the plaits on to a hook in the window, and when the prince came and called out,

"Rapunzel, Rapunzel,
  Let down your golden hair,"

she let them down, and the prince climbed up as usual. Instead of his beloved Rapunzel he found the old witch, who fixed her evil, glittering eyes on him, and cried mockingly, "Ah, ah! You thought to find your lady love, but Rapunzel is lost to you forever – you will never see her more."

The prince was beside himself with grief, and in

his despair he jumped right down from the tower. Though he escaped with his life, the thorns among which he fell pierced his eyes. Then he wandered, blind and miserable, through the wood, eating nothing but roots and berries, and weeping for the loss of his lovely bride.

So he wandered about for some years, as wretched and unhappy as he could be, and at last he came to the desert place where Rapunzel was living. Suddenly he heard a voice that seemed strangely familiar to him. He walked eagerly in the direction of the sound, and when he was quite close, Rapunzel recognized him and hugged him and wept. Two of her tears touched his eyes, and in a moment they became quite clear again, and he saw as well as he had ever done. Then he led her to his kingdom, where they were received and welcomed with great joy, and they lived happily ever after.

The Mandarin
and the
Butterfly

From *American Fairy Tales* by L Frank Baum

A mandarin once lived in Kiang-ho who was so exceedingly cross and disagreeable that everyone hated him. He snarled and stormed at every person he met, and was never known to laugh or be merry under any circumstances. He hated boys and girls especially, for they jeered and made fun of him.

When he had become so unpopular that no one would speak to him, the emperor heard about it and commanded him to emigrate to America. This suited the mandarin very well, but before he left

China he stole the Great Book of Magic that belonged to the wise magician Haot-sai. Then, gathering up his little store of money, he took ship for America. He settled in a city of the middle west and started a laundry.

One day, as the ugly one was ironing in the basement of his shop, he looked up and saw a crowd of childish faces pressed against the window. He tried to drive them away, but as soon as he returned to his work they were back at the window again, mischievously smiling down upon him. The mandarin uttered horrid words in the Manchu language and made fierce gestures, but this did no good at all. The children stayed as long as they pleased, and they came again the very next day as soon as school was over, and likewise the next day, and the next. For they saw their presence at the window bothered the Chinaman and were delighted accordingly.

The following day being Sunday the children did not appear, but as the mandarin worked in his little

shop, a big butterfly flew in at the open door and
fluttered about the room.

The mandarin closed the door and chased the
butterfly until he caught it. He pinned it against the
wall by sticking two pins through its beautiful
wings. This did not hurt the butterfly, there being
no feeling in its wings, but it made him a safe
prisoner. This butterfly was of large size and its
wings were exquisitely marked by gorgeous colours
laid out in regular designs, just like the stained glass
windows of a cathedral.

The mandarin now opened his wooden chest and drew forth the Great Book of Magic he had stolen from Haot-sai. Turning the pages slowly he came to a passage describing how to understand the language of butterflies. This he read carefully, and then mixed a magic formula in a tin cup and drank it down with a wry face. Immediately thereafter he spoke to the butterfly in its own language.

"You are my prisoner," said the mandarin. "If I please I can kill you, or leave you on the wall to starve to death. But if you promise to obey me for a time and carry out my instructions, I will give you a long and pleasant life by means of powerful magic."

"I promise," answered the butterfly. "For even as your slave I will get some enjoyment out of life. But if you kill me – that is the end of everything!"

"Then, listen! You know children, do you not?"

"Yes, I know them. They chase me, and try to catch me, as you have done," replied the butterfly.

"They mock me and jeer at me through the window," continued the mandarin. "Therefore, they are your enemies and mine! But with your aid and the help of the magic book we shall have a fine revenge for their insults."

"I don't care much for revenge," said the butterfly. "They are but children, and it is natural they should wish to catch such a beautiful creature as I am."

"Nevertheless, I care! And you must obey me," retorted the mandarin, harshly. "I, at least, will have my revenge."

Then he stuck a drop of molasses upon the wall beside the butterfly's head and said, "Eat that, while I read my book and prepare my magic formula."

So the butterfly feasted upon the molasses and the mandarin studied his book, after which he began to mix a magic compound in the tin cup.

When the mixture was ready he released the butterfly from the wall and said to it, "I command you to dip your two front feet into this magic compound and then fly away until you meet a child. Fly close, whether it be a boy or a girl, and touch the child upon its forehead with your feet. Whosoever is thus touched, the book declares, will at once become a pig, and will remain such forever after. Then return to me and dip you legs afresh in the contents of this cup. So shall all my enemies, the children, become miserable swine, while no one will think of accusing me of the sorcery."

"Very well, since such is your command, I obey," said the butterfly. Then it dipped its front legs, which were the shortest of the six, into the contents of the tin cup, and flew out of the door and away over the houses to the edge of the town. There it alighted in a flower garden and soon forgot all about its mission to turn children into swine.

In going from flower to flower it soon brushed the magic compound from its legs, so that when the sun began to set and the butterfly finally remembered its master, the mandarin, it could not have injured a child had it tried. But it did not intend to try.

'That horrid old Chinaman,' it thought, 'hates

children and wishes to destroy them. But I rather like children myself and shall not harm them. Of course I must return to my master, for he is a magician, and would seek me out and kill me. But I can deceive him about this matter easily enough.'

When the butterfly flew in at the door of the mandarin's laundry, the Chinaman asked, eagerly, "Well, did you meet a child?"

"I did," replied the butterfly. "It was a pretty, golden-haired girl – but now 'tis a grunting pig!"

"Good! Good!" cried the mandarin, dancing joyfully about the room. "You shall have molasses for your supper, and tomorrow you must change two children into pigs."

The butterfly did not reply, and it ate the molasses in silence.

Next morning, by the mandarin's command, the butterfly dipped its legs in the mixture and flew away in search of children.

When it came to the edge of the town it noticed a pig in a sty, and alighting upon the rail of the sty it looked down at the creature and thought, 'If I could change a child into a pig by touching it with the magic compound, what could I change a pig into?'

Being curious to determine this fine point in sorcery the butterfly fluttered down and touched its front feet to the pig's nose. Instantly the animal disappeared, and in its place was a shock-headed, dirty-looking boy, which sprang straight from the sty and ran down the road uttering loud whoops.

"That's funny," said the butterfly to itself. "The mandarin would be very angry with me if he knew of this, for I have liberated one more of the creatures that bother him."

Then it flew into a rose bush, where it remained comfortably until evening. At sundown it returned to its master.

"Have you changed two of them into pigs?" the mandarin asked at once.

"I have," lied the butterfly.

"Good! Good!" screamed the mandarin, in an ecstasy of delight. "Change every child you meet into a pig!"

"Very well," answered the butterfly, quietly, and ate its supper of molasses.

Several days were passed by the butterfly in the same manner. It fluttered aimlessly about the flower gardens while the sun shone, and returned at night to the mandarin with false tales of turning children into swine. Sometimes it would be one child that was transformed, sometimes it would be two, and occasionally three, but the mandarin always greeted the butterfly's report with intense delight and gave him molasses for supper.

One evening, however, the butterfly thought it might be well to vary the report, so that the mandarin might not grow suspicious. When its master asked what child had been changed into a pig that day the lying creature answered, "It was a Chinese boy."

This angered the mandarin, who was in an especially cross mood. He spitefully snapped at the butterfly with his finger, and nearly broke its beautiful wing, for he forgot that Chinese boys had once mocked him and only remembered his hatred for American boys.

The butterfly became very indignant at this abuse from the mandarin. It refused to eat its molasses and sulked all evening, for it had grown to hate the mandarin as much as the mandarin hated children.

When morning came it was still trembling with indignation, but the mandarin cried out, "Make haste, miserable slave, for today you must change four children into pigs, to make up for yesterday."

The butterfly did not reply. His little black eyes were sparkling wickedly, and no sooner had he dipped his feet into the magic compound than he flew full in the mandarin's face, and touched him upon his ugly, flat forehead.

Soon after a gentleman came into the room for his laundry. The mandarin was not there, but running around the place was a repulsive, scrawny pig, which squealed most miserably.

The butterfly flew away to a brook and washed from its feet all traces of the magic compound. When night came it slept in a rose bush.

Hansel and Grettel

Retold by Andrew Lang in his *Blue Fairy Book*,
after the Brothers Grimm

Once upon a time there dwelt on the outskirts of a large forest a poor woodcutter with his wife and two children – the boy was called Hansel and the girl, Grettel. He had always little to live on, and a time came when he couldn't even provide them with daily bread. One night, unable to sleep with worry, he sighed and said to the children's stepmother, "What's to become of us? How are we to live?"

"I'll tell you what, husband," answered the woman, "early tomorrow morning we'll take the children out into the thickest part of the wood and leave them."

"No, wife," said her husband, "how could I?"

"Then we must all four die of hunger," said she, and she nagged and moaned till he agreed.

The children had been awake with hunger and had heard everything. Grettel wept bitterly, but Hansel got up, slipped on his coat, opened the back door and stole out. The moon was shining and the white pebbles that lay in front of the house glittered like silver. Hansel filled his pocket with as many of them as he could. Then he went back and said to Grettel, "Be comforted, my dear little sister, and go to sleep. I have a way to escape."

At daybreak, the woman came and woke the children. "Get up, we're all going to fetch wood," she commanded. She gave them each a bit of bread and said, "There's something for your lunch – it's all you're getting." Then they all set out together.

After they had walked for a little, Hansel stood and looked back at the house, and this he repeated again and again. His father observed him, and said, "Hansel, what are you gazing at?"

"Oh Father," said Hansel, "I am looking back at my white kitten, which is sitting on the roof, waving me farewell." However Hansel had not looked back at his kitten, but each time had dropped one of the white pebbles out of his pocket onto the path.

When they had reached the middle of the forest and collected brushwood for a fire the woman said, "Now sit down, children, and rest. We are going to cut wood, but when we've finished we'll come back and fetch you."

Hansel and Grettel sat down beside the fire, and at midday ate their little bits of bread. When they had waited for a long time their eyes closed and they fell fast asleep.

It was pitch dark when they awoke. Grettel began to cry, and said, "How are we ever going to get out of the wood?"

But Hansel comforted her, saying, "Only wait, Grettel, till the full moon is up."

Then, he took his sister by the hand and followed the pebbles, which shone like bright coins in the moonlight and showed them the path. They walked on through the night, and at daybreak reached their home again – to the stepmother's great annoyance and the father's huge relief.

Not long afterwards, one night the children again overheard their stepmother force their father to agree to abandon them in the forest. Hansel got up and wanted to go out and pick up pebbles again, as he had done the first time, but the woman had barred the door, and he couldn't get out.

At early dawn the woman came and made the children get up. They received their bit of bread, but it was even smaller than before. On the way into the wood Hansel crumbled it in his pocket, and every few minutes he stood still and dropped a crumb on the ground. "Hansel, what are you stopping and looking about for?" said the father.

"I'm looking back at my little pigeon, which is sitting on the roof waving me farewell," answered Hansel. But Hansel was gradually throwing all his crumbs on the path.

The woman led the children still deeper into the forest. Then a big fire was lit again, and she said, "Just sit down there, children. We're going into the forest to cut down wood, and in the evening when we're finished we'll come back to fetch you."

At midday Grettel divided her bread with Hansel, for he had strewn his all along their path. Then they fell asleep and didn't awake till it was pitch dark and they were still all alone. Hansel comforted his sister, saying, "Only wait, Grettel, till the moon rises, then we shall see the breadcrumbs I scattered along the path. They will show us the way back to the house."

When the moon appeared they got up, but they found no crumbs, for the birds had picked them all up. "Never mind," said Hansel to Grettel, "you'll see we'll find a way out." But all the same they did not. They wandered about the whole night, and the next day, but they could not find a path out of the wood. They were very hungry, too, for they had nothing to eat but a few berries they found.

On the third morning they got deeper and deeper into the wood, and now they felt that if help did not come to them soon they must perish. At midday they stumbled across a little house, and when they came quite near they saw that it was made of bread and roofed with cakes, while the windows were made of transparent sugar. Hansel stretched up his hand and broke off a little bit of the roof to see what it was like, and Grettel went to the window and began to nibble at it.

Suddenly the door opened, and an ancient dame leaning on a staff hobbled out. Hansel and Grettel were terrified, but the old woman said, "Oh, ho! You dear children, come in and stay with me, no ill shall befall you." She took them both by the hand and let them into the house. Then she laid a most sumptuous dinner before them – milk and sugared pancakes, with apples and nuts. After they had finished, two little white beds were prepared for them, and when Hansel and Grettel lay down in them they felt as if they had got into heaven.

The old woman had appeared to be most friendly, but she was really an old witch who had only built the little bread house in order to lure the children in. For when anyone came into her power

she killed, cooked and ate them!

Early in the morning, before the children were awake, she rose up and seized Hansel with her bony hand and carried him into a stable, and barred the door on him – he might scream as much as he liked, it did him no good. Then she went to Grettel, shook her awake and cried, "Get up, you lazy-bones, fetch water and cook something for your brother. When he's fat I'll eat him up." Grettel began to cry bitterly, but it was no use – she had to do what the wicked witch bade her.

So the best food was cooked for poor Hansel, but Grettel got nothing but crab shells. Every morning the old woman hobbled out to the stable and cried, "Hansel, put out your finger, that I may feel if you are getting fat." But Hansel always stretched out a bone, and the old dame, whose eyes were dim, couldn't see it. The witch always thought it was Hansel's finger and wondered why he fattened so slowly. When four weeks had passed and Hansel still remained thin, she lost patience and decided to wait no longer.

"Grettel," she called, "be quick and get some water. Hansel may be fat or thin, I'm going to kill him tomorrow and cook him."

Oh, how the poor little sister sobbed! Early in the morning she had to go out and hang up the kettle full of water and light the fire.

"First we'll bake," said the old dame. "I've heated the oven already and kneaded the dough." She pushed Grettel out to the blazing oven. "Creep in," said the witch, "and see if it's hot enough, so that we can shove in the bread." For when she had got Grettel in she meant to close the oven and let the girl bake, that she might eat her up too.

But Grettel knew what the old dame had in mind, and said, "I don't know how I'm to do it. How do I get in?"

"You silly goose!" said the witch. "The opening is big enough. See, I could get in myself," and she crawled toward it and poked her head into the oven. Then Grettel shoved her right in, shut the iron door, and drew the bolt. Gracious, how the witch yelled! It was quite horrible. But Grettel fled, and the wretched old woman was left to perish.

Grettel flew straight to Hansel, opened the stable door, and cried, "Hansel, we are free! The old witch is dead." Then Hansel sprang like a bird out of an opened cage. How they rejoiced and jumped for joy and kissed one another! They went back into the old hag's house, and here they found, in every corner of the room, boxes with pearls and precious stones, which they crammed into their clothes.

"Now," said Hansel, "let's get well away."

When they had wandered about for some hours, the wood became more and more familiar to them, and at length they saw their father's house in the distance. Then they set off to run and, bounding into the room, fell on their father with joy. He had been despairing since he left them in the wood, and the wicked stepmother had died. Grettel shook out her apron so that the pearls and precious stones rolled about the room, and Hansel threw down one handful after the other out of his pocket. Thus all their troubles were ended, and they lived happily ever after.

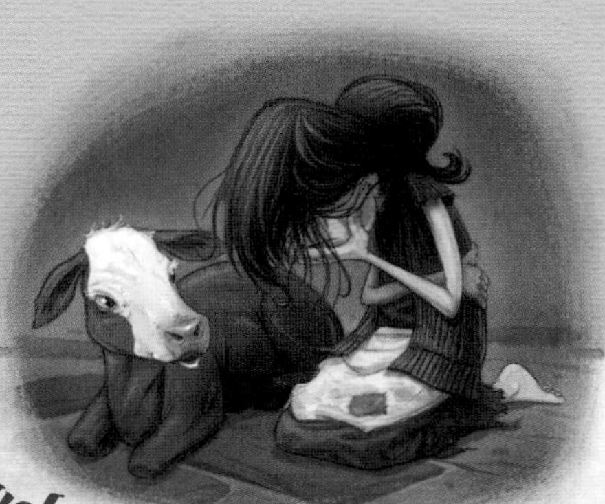

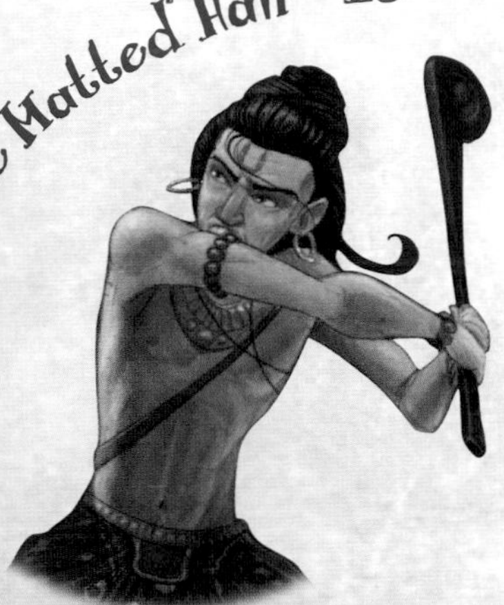

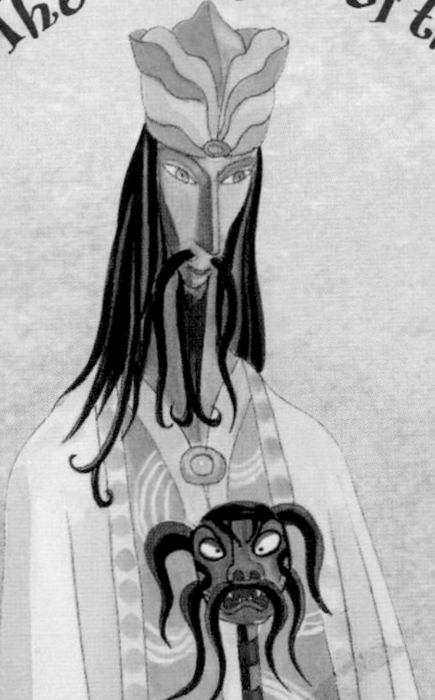

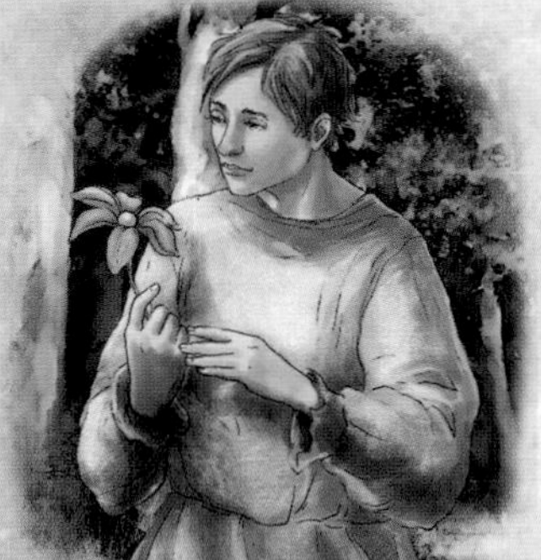

DÄRING DEEDS

103

Rushen Coatie

A Cinderella story, from *More English Fairy Tales*
by Joseph Jacobs

There was once a king and a queen who had a bonny girl. But the queen died, telling the girl on her deathbed, "My dear, after I am gone, there will come to you a little red calf, and whenever you want anything, speak to it, and it will give it you."

Now, after a while, the king married again. His wife was ill-natured, and she had three ugly daughters of her own, who hated the king's daughter. So they took all her fine clothes away from her, and gave her only a coat made of rushes. They called her Rushen Coatie, and made her sit in the kitchen nook, amid the ashes.

When dinnertime came, the nasty stepmother sent her out a thimbleful of broth, a grain of barley, a thread of meat and a crumb of bread. But when she had eaten this, she was just as hungry as before, so she said to herself, "Oh, how I wish I had something to eat!"

Just then, who should come in but a little red calf, and it said to her, "Put your finger into my left ear." She did so, and found some nice bread. Then the calf told her to put her finger into its right ear, and she found there some cheese, and made a right good meal. And so it went on from day to day.

Now the king's wife thought Rushen Coatie would soon die from the lack of food, and she was surprised to see her as lively and healthy as ever. So she set one of her ugly daughters to watch at meal times. The daughter soon found out that the red calf gave food to Rushen Coatie, and told her mother. So her mother went to the king and told him she was longing to have some meat from a red calf. Then the king sent for his butcher, and had the little calf killed.

When Rushen Coatie heard of it, she sat down and wept by its side, but the dead calf said,

"Take me up, bone by bone,
And put me beneath yon grey stone.
When there is aught you want
Tell it me, and that I'll grant."

So she did so, but could not find one of the calf's leg bones.

Now the very next Sunday, all the folk were going to church in their best clothes, but the three ugly sisters told Rushen Coatie she must stay at home and make the dinner.

When they all went to church, Rushen Coatie sat down and wept, but looking up, who should she see coming in limping, with one leg missing, but the dear red calf? And the red calf said to her, "Do not sit there weeping, but put on these clothes, and above all, put on this pair of glass slippers, and go on your way to church."

"But what will become of the dinner?" asked Rushen Coatie.

"Oh, do not worry about that," said the red calf.

So Rushen Coatie went off to church, and she was the grandest and finest lady there. Now there happened to be a young prince at the church, and he fell at once in love with her. But she came away before service was over, and was home before the rest, and had off with her fine clothes and on with her rushen coatie. She found the little red calf had covered the table, and the dinner was ready, and everything was in good order when the rest came home.

The three sisters said to Rushen Coatie, "Oh, lassie, if you had seen the bonny fine lady in church today, that the young prince fell in love with!"

Then she said, "Oh! I wish you would let me go with you to the church next time."

But they said, "What should the likes of you do at church, nasty thing? The kitchen nook is good enough for you."

So the next time they all went to church, Rushen Coatie was left behind to make dinner. But the red calf came to her again, gave her finer clothes than before, and she went to church. All the world was looking at her, and wondering where such a grand lady came from, and the prince fell more in love with her than ever before, and tried to find out where she went to. But she was too quick for him, and got home long before the rest, and the red calf had the dinner all ready.

The next Sunday the calf dressed her in even grander clothes than before, and she went to the church. The young prince was there again, and this time he put a guard at the door to keep her, but she took a hop and a run and jumped over their heads, and as she did so, down fell one of her glass slippers. She didn't wait to pick it up, but off she ran home, as fast as she could go, on with the rushen coatie, and the calf had all things ready.

The young prince put out a proclamation that whoever could put on the glass slipper should be his bride. All the ladies of his court went and tried to put on the slipper. They tried and tried, but it was too small for them all. Then he ordered one of his ambassadors to ride through the kingdom and find an owner for the glass shoe. He rode to town and castle, and made all the ladies try to put on the shoe. Many a one tried to get it on that she might be the prince's bride. But no, it wouldn't do, and many a one wept, because she couldn't get on the little glass slipper.

The ambassador rode on and on till he came at last to the house where there were the three ugly sisters. The first two tried to put on the glass slipper and it wouldn't do, and the queen, mad with spite, cut off the toes and heels of the third sister. Then she could put the slipper on, and the prince was brought to marry her, for he had to keep his promise. The ugly sister was dressed all in her best and was put up behind the prince on horseback. Then off they rode in great gallantry. But pride must have a fall, for as they rode along, a raven sang out of a bush,

"Cut Heels and Toes
  Behind the young prince rides.
  But Pretty Feet and Little Feet
  Behind the cauldron bides."

"What's that the birdie sings?" said the prince.

"Nasty, lying thing," said the stepsister, "never mind what it is singing."

But the prince looked down and saw her feet dripping with blood, so he rode back and put her down. Then he said, "There must be someone that the slipper has not been tried on."

"Oh, no," said they, "there's none but a dirty thing that sits in the kitchen nook and wears a rushen coatie."

The prince was determined to try the slipper on Rushen Coatie, but she ran away to the grey stone, where the red calf dressed her in her bravest dress. And then she went to the prince and the slipper jumped out of his pocket onto her foot, fitting her perfectly. So the prince married her that very day, and they lived happily ever after.

The Demon

with the

Matted Hair

From *Indian Fairy Stories*
by Joseph Jacobs

Once upon a time, when Brahmadatta was King of Benares, his chief queen gave birth to a son who was actually a holy being called the Bodhisatta. On the baby's name day the king asked eight hundred wise men called Brahmans about his lucky marks. The Brahmans replied, "Full of goodness, great king, is your son, and when you die he will become king. He shall be famous and renowned for his skill with the five weapons, and shall be the chief man in all India."

On hearing what the Brahmans had to say, the

king and queen gave their son the name of the
Prince of the Five Weapons – sword, spear, bow,
club and shield.

The Bodhisatta grew up tall and strong, wise and
good, and when he was sixteen years old, the king
said to him, "My son, you must go and complete
your education."

"Who shall be my teacher?" the lad asked.

"Go, my son. In the kingdom of Candahar, in the
city of Takkasila, is a far-famed teacher from whom
I wish you to learn. Take this, and give it to him for
a fee." With that the king gave his son a thousand
pieces of money and dismissed him.

The lad departed and was educated by this
teacher, receiving the five weapons from him as a
gift. When his studies were complete, the lad bade
his teacher farewell, and began his journey back to
Benares, armed with the five weapons.

On his way he came to a forest inhabited by the
Demon with the Matted Hair. As he was entering
the forest some men saw him, and cried out, "Hello,

young sir, keep clear of that wood! There's a demon in it called he of the Matted Hair. He kills every man he sees!" And they tried to stop him. But the Bodhisatta, having confidence in himself, went straight on, fearless as a lion.

When he reached mid-forest the demon showed itself. It made itself as tall as a palm tree. Its head was the size of a pagoda, its eyes as big as saucers, and it had two tusks. It had the face of a hawk, a striped belly, and blue hands and feet.

"Where are you going?" it shouted. "Stop! You'll make a meal for me!"

Said the Bodhisatta, "Demon, beware!" With this, he fitted to his bow an arrow dipped in deadly poison, and let it fly. The arrow stuck fast in the demon's hair. Then he shot and shot, till he had shot away fifty arrows – and they all stuck in the demon's hair. The demon snapped them all off short, and threw them down at its feet. Then it came up to the Bodhisatta, who drew his sword and struck the demon, threatening him the while. His sword stuck in the demon's hair! The Bodhisatta struck him with his spear – that stuck too! He struck him with his club – and that stuck too!

"You, demon!" the Bodhisatta cried. "Did you never hear of me before – the Prince of the Five Weapons? This day will I pound you to powder!" And he hit at the demon with his right hand. It stuck fast in its hair! He hit it with his left hand – that stuck too! With his right foot he kicked it – that stuck too. Then with his left – and that stuck too! Then he butted at the demon with his head, crying, "I'll grind you to dust!" And his head stuck fast like the rest.

Thus the Bodhisatta was five times snared, caught fast in five places. Yet he felt no fear and he was not even nervous.

The demon thought to itself, 'Here's a lion of a man! A noble man! Here he is, caught by a demon like me, yet he will not fear me a bit. Since I have ravaged this road, I never saw such a man.'

The demon asked, "Why is it, young sir, that you

are not at all frightened of me?"

"Why should I fear, demon?" the Bodhisatta replied. "In one life a man can die but once. Besides, in my belly is a thunderbolt – if you eat me, you will never be able to digest it. This will tear your innards into little bits and kill you, so we shall both perish. That is why I fear nothing." The Bodhisatta meant the weapon of knowledge that he had within him.

When it heard this, the demon thought, 'This young man speaks the truth. A piece of the flesh of such a lion-man as he would be too much for me to digest, if it were no bigger than a kidney bean. I'll let him go!' So, being frightened to death, it let go of the Bodhisatta, saying, "Young sir, I will not eat you up. I set you free!"

And the Bodhisatta said, "Demon, I will go, as you say. You were born a demon, devourer of the flesh and gore of others, because you did wicked things in former lives. And if you go on doing wicked things, you will go from darkness to darkness." Then he told the demon about the punishments that awaited evil creatures, and the rewards that awaited good beings. The demon vowed before the gods to change his ways.

Then the prince went on to Benares, armed with his five weapons, and became a king who ruled long and righteously.

The Dragon of the North

A myth from northern lands,
retold by Andrew Lang from the *Yellow Fairy Book*

Very long ago, there lived a terrible dragon that came out of the North and laid waste whole tracts of country, devouring both men and beasts. This dragon had a body like an ox, and legs like a frog, two short forelegs, and two long ones behind, and besides that it had a tail like a serpent. When it moved it jumped like a frog, and with every spring it covered half a mile of ground. Nothing could hunt it because its whole body was covered with scales, which were harder than stone or metal. Its two great eyes shone by night, and even by day, like the brightest lamps, and anyone who had the ill luck to look into them became bewitched, and was obliged to rush of his own accord into the dragon's jaws. In this way the dragon was able to feed upon both men and beasts without the least trouble to itself, as it needed not to move from the spot where it was lying. Its habit was to remain for several years in the same place, and it would not move on till the whole neighbourhood was eaten up.

All the neighbouring kings had offered rich rewards to anyone who could destroy the dragon, either by force or enchantment, and many had tried their luck, but all had failed miserably. However, there was a saying that the dragon might be overcome by one who possessed King Solomon's signet ring, upon which a secret writing was engraved. This inscription would enable anyone who was wise enough to interpret it to find out how the dragon could be destroyed. Only no one knew where the ring was hidden.

At last a young man, with a good heart and plenty of courage, set out to search for the ring. He took his way towards the sunrise, because he knew that all the wisdom of old time comes from the East. After some years he met with a famous Eastern magician, and asked for his advice in the matter. The magician answered, "Mortal men have but little wisdom, and can give you no help. The birds of the air would be better guides to you if you could learn their language. I can help you to understand it if you will stay with me a few days." The youth thankfully accepted the magician's offer. Each day for three days, he drank nine spoonfuls of a powerful potion, which made him able to understand the language of birds.

From then on, the youth never felt lonely as he walked along. He always had company, because he understood the language of birds, and in this way he learned many things that mere human knowledge could never have taught him.

One afternoon, when he had sat down under a tree in a forest to eat his lunch, he heard two gaily-plumaged birds discussing how he could only find King Solomon's lost ring if he sought help from the witch-maiden, who at dusk would wash her face in a magic spring to stay ever young and beautiful. The birds were going to watch, so the youth resolved to follow the birds to the spring.

When the birds flew away, the youth's heart beat with anxiety lest he should lose sight of his guides, but by running as hard as he could he managed to keep them in view until they again perched upon a tree. The young man ran after them until he was

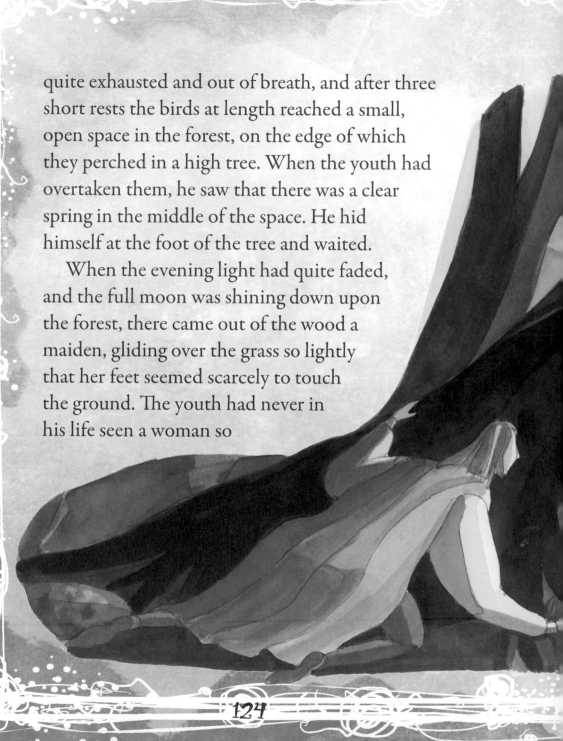

quite exhausted and out of breath, and after three short rests the birds at length reached a small, open space in the forest, on the edge of which they perched in a high tree. When the youth had overtaken them, he saw that there was a clear spring in the middle of the space. He hid himself at the foot of the tree and waited.

When the evening light had quite faded, and the full moon was shining down upon the forest, there came out of the wood a maiden, gliding over the grass so lightly that her feet seemed scarcely to touch the ground. The youth had never in his life seen a woman so beautiful. She went to the spring, looked up to the full moon, then knelt down and bathed her face nine times. She then looked up to the moon again and walked nine times round the well, singing. Then she dried her face with her long hair, and was about to go away, when her eye suddenly fell upon the spot where the young man was hiding. The youth knew he had been discovered and rose, saying, "Forgive me, beautiful maiden, if I have offended by watching you."

The maiden answered kindly, "Come and spend this night in my house. You will sleep better on a pillow than on damp moss."

The youth hesitated, but he heard the birds saying from the top of the tree, "Go where she calls you, but take care to give no blood, or you will sell your soul." So the youth went with her, and soon they reached a beautiful garden, where stood a splendid house, which glittered in the moonlight as if it was built out of gold and silver. When the youth entered he found many splendid chambers, each one finer than the last. Hundreds of candles burned upon golden candlesticks, and shed a light like the brightest day.

At length they reached a chamber where a table was spread with the most costly dishes. At the table were placed two chairs, one of silver, the other of gold. The maiden seated herself upon the golden chair, and offered the silver one to her companion. They were served by maidens dressed in white, whose feet made no sound as they moved about, and not a word was spoken during the meal. Afterwards the youth and the witch-maiden talked pleasantly together, until a woman, dressed in red, came in to remind them that it was bedtime. The youth was now shown into another room, containing a silken bed with down cushions, where he slept delightfully, yet he seemed to hear a voice near his bed that repeated to him, "Remember to give no blood!"

The next morning the maiden asked him whether he would not like to marry her and stay with her always in this wonderful place. The youth was tempted, but he remembered how the birds had called her a witch, and their warning always sounded in his ears. Therefore he answered cautiously and asked for some days to consider the matter. The maiden agreed, and to make the time pass pleasantly, she took the youth over every part of her beautiful dwelling, and showed him all her splendid treasures.

One day the maiden took him into a secret chamber, where a little gold box was standing on a silver table. Pointing to the box, she said, "Here is my greatest treasure, whose like is not to be found in the whole world. It is a precious gold ring. When you marry me, I will give you this ring as a marriage gift, and it will make you the happiest of mortal men. But in order that our love may last forever, you must give me for the ring three drops of blood from the little finger of your left hand."

When the youth heard these words a cold shudder ran over him, for he remembered that his soul was at stake. He was cunning enough, however, to conceal his feelings and to make no direct answer, but he only asked the maiden, as if carelessly, what was remarkable about the ring.

She answered, "No mortal is able entirely to understand the power of this ring, because no one thoroughly understands the secret signs engraved upon it. But even with my half-knowledge I can work great wonders. If I put the ring upon the little finger of my left hand, then I can fly like a bird through the air wherever I wish to go. If I put it on the fourth finger of my left hand I am invisible, and

I can see everything that passes around me, though no one can see me. If I put the ring upon the middle finger of my left hand, then neither fire nor water nor any sharp weapon can hurt me. If I put it on the forefinger of my left hand, then I can produce whatever I wish. I can in a single moment build houses or anything I desire. Finally, as long as I wear the ring on the thumb of my left hand, that hand is so strong that it can break down rocks and walls.

"Besides these, the ring has other secret signs that, as I said, no one can understand. No doubt it contains secrets of great importance. The ring formerly belonged to King Solomon, the wisest of kings, during whose reign the wisest men lived. But it is not known whether this ring was ever made by mortal hands – it is supposed that an angel gave it to wise King Solomon."

Then the youth had a cunning idea. "I do not think it possible that the ring can have all the power you say it has," he said. "Do let me try to see if I can do these wonderful things."

The maiden, suspecting no treachery, gave him the magic ring.

The youth asked her to remind him what finger he must put the ring on so that he could fly.

"Oh, the little finger of your left hand," the maiden answered, laughing.

The youth did so, and he soared into the air just like a bird.

When the maiden saw him flying away she thought he was playing, but the young man never came back. Then the maiden saw she was deceived, and bitterly repented that she had ever trusted him with the ring.

The young man never halted in his flight until he reached the dwelling of the wise magician who had taught him the language of birds. The magician delightedly set to work at once to interpret the secret signs engraved upon the ring, but it took him seven weeks to make them out clearly. Then he told the youth he must have an iron horse cast, with little wheels under each foot. He must have huge iron chains and pegs made, and he must be armed with a spear as long and thick as a tree, which he would be able to wield by means of the magic ring upon his left thumb. And he told the youth how to use these to defeat the dragon.

The young man thanked the magician sincerely and quickly flew home through the air. After some weeks, he heard people say that the terrible Dragon of the North was not far off. The king announced publicly that he would give his daughter in marriage, as well as a large part of his kingdom, to whoever should free the country from the dragon. The youth went to the king and everything was prepared as he requested.

The young man rode out upon the iron horse to meet the dragon, pushing the spear against the ground, as if he were pushing off a boat from the land. The dragon had his monstrous jaws wide open! The youth trembled with horror and his blood ran cold, yet he did not lose his courage. Holding the iron spear upright in his hand, he brought it down with all his might right through the dragon's lower jaw. Then quick as lightning he sprang from his horse before the dragon had time to shut his mouth. A fearful clap like thunder, which could be heard for miles around, now warned him that the dragon's jaws had closed upon the spear.

When the youth turned round he saw the point of the spear sticking up high above the dragon's upper jaw, and knew that the other end must be fastened firmly to the ground. But the dragon had got its teeth fixed in the iron horse, which was now useless. The youth now hastened to fasten down the chains to the ground by means of the enormous iron pegs that he had provided.

The death struggle of the dragon lasted three days and three nights. In its writhing it beat its tail so violently against the ground, that at ten miles away the earth trembled as if with an earthquake. When the dragon at length lost power to move its tail, the youth, with the help of the ring, took up a stone that twenty ordinary men could not have moved. He hit the dragon on the head with it, so that it lay lifeless before him.

You can fancy how great was the rejoicing when the news was spread that the terrible dragon was dead. Its conqueror was received into the city with as much celebration as if he had been the mightiest of kings. The king's daughter was delighted to marry the hero, and a magnificent wedding was celebrated. But everyone forgot amid the general joy that they ought to have buried the dragon's monstrous body, for it began to have such a bad smell that the whole air was poisoned, which destroyed many hundreds of people.

In this distress, the king's son-in-law resolved to

seek help once more from the Eastern magician, to whom he at once travelled through the air in the form of a bird. However, the witch-maiden had discovered by magic where the youth and her ring were. She changed herself into an eagle and watched in the air until the bird came in sight, then she pounced upon him and tore the ring from the ribbon he wore around his neck. Then the eagle flew down to the earth with her prey, and the two stood face to face once more in human form.

"Now, villain, you are in my power and you must pay!" cried the witch-maiden. She put the ring upon her left thumb, lifted the young man with onc hand, and walked away with him to a deep cave. The maiden chained the young man's hands and feet to the rock so that he could not escape and declared, "Here you shall remain until you die. I will bring you enough food to prevent you dying of hunger, but you need never hope for freedom again." And with these words she left him.

The old king and his daughter waited anxiously

for many weeks for the prince's return, but no news of him arrived. They sent messengers far and wide to look for him.

After searching for seven long years, by good luck they met with the old magician who had interpreted the signs on King Solomon's ring. The magician soon found out what they wished to know, and went himself to the cave where the unfortunate prince was chained up. The magician released him by the help of powerful magic, and took care of the prince until he became strong enough to travel. When he reached home he found that the old king had died, so that he was now raised to the throne. And now after his long suffering came prosperity, which lasted to the end of his life. But he never got back the magic ring, nor has it ever again been seen by mortal eyes.

Jorinda and Jorindel

By the Brothers Grimm

There was once an old castle that stood in the middle of a deep, gloomy wood, and in the castle lived an old fairy. Now this fairy could take any shape she pleased. All day long she flew about in the form of an owl, or crept about like a cat, but at night she always became an old woman again. When any young man came within a hundred paces of her castle, he became quite fixed, and could not move a step till she came and set him free. But when any pretty maiden came within that space she was changed into a bird, and the fairy put her into a cage, and hung her up in a chamber in the castle. There were seven hundred of these cages hanging in the castle, and all with beautiful birds in them.

Now there was once a maiden whose name was Jorinda. She was prettier than all the pretty girls that ever were seen before. A shepherd lad, whose name was Jorindel, was very fond of her, and they were soon to be married. One day they went to walk in the wood, and Jorindel said, "We must take care that we don't go too near to the fairy's castle."

It was a beautiful evening. The last rays of the setting sun shone bright through the long stems of the trees upon the green underwood beneath, and turtle doves sang from the tall birches. Jorinda sat down to gaze upon the sun and Jorindel sat by her side. And both felt sad, they knew not why, but it seemed as if they were to be parted from one another forever. They had wandered a long way, and when they looked to see which way they should go home, they found themselves at a loss to know what path to take.

The sun was setting fast. Jorindel suddenly looked behind him, and saw through the bushes that they had, without knowing it, sat down close under the old walls of the castle. Then he shrank for fear, turned pale and trembled.

Jorinda was singing, when her song stopped suddenly. Jorindel turned to see the reason, and beheld his Jorinda changed into a nightingale! Jorindel could not move – he was fixed as a stone,

and could neither weep, nor speak, nor stir hand or foot.

Now the sun went quite down and the gloomy night came. The old fairy came forth, pale and meagre, with staring eyes, and a nose and chin that almost met one another. She mumbled something to herself, seized the nightingale, and went away with it in her hand.

Poor Jorindel saw the nightingale was gone – but what could he do? He could not speak, he could not move from the spot where he stood. At last the fairy came back and suddenly Jorindel found himself free. Then he fell on his knees before the fairy, and pleaded with her to give him back his dear Jorinda. But she laughed at him, said he would never see her again, and then went on her way.

He prayed, he wept, he sorrowed, but all in vain. "Alas!" he said. "What will become of me?" He could not go back to his own home, so he went to a nearby village, and employed himself in keeping sheep. Many a time did he walk round and round as near to the hated castle as he dared go, but all in vain – he heard and saw nothing of Jorinda.

At last Jorindel dreamed one night that he found a beautiful purple flower, and that in the middle of it lay a costly pearl. And he dreamed that he plucked the flower, and went with it in his hand into the castle. He dreamed that everything he touched with it was disenchanted, and that there he found his Jorinda.

In the morning when he awoke, he began to search over hill and dale for this pretty flower. And eight long days he sought for it in vain, but on the ninth day, early in the morning, he found the beautiful purple flower. In the middle of it was a large dewdrop, as big as a costly pearl. Then he plucked the flower, and travelled day and night, till

he came again to the castle. He walked nearer than a hundred paces to it, and yet he did not become fixed as before, but found that he could go quite close up to the door. Jorindel was very glad indeed to see this. Then he touched the door with the flower, and it sprang open. He went in through the court and listened, hearing many birds singing.

At last he came to the chamber where the fairy sat, with the seven hundred birds singing in the seven hundred cages. When the fairy saw Jorindel she was very angry and screamed with rage. But she could not come within two yards of him, for the flower he held in his hand was his safeguard. He looked around at the birds in the cages, but there were many, many nightingales, and how then should he find out which one was his Jorinda?

While he was thinking what to do, he saw the fairy had taken down one of the cages, and was making her way off through the door. He ran after her, touched the cage with the flower, and Jorinda stood before him. She threw her arms round his

neck, looking as beautiful as ever, as beautiful as when they walked together in the wood.

Then he touched all the other birds with the flower, so that they all took their old forms again. And he took Jorinda home, where they were married, and lived happily together many years. And so did a good many other lads, whose maidens had been forced to sing in the old fairy's cages by themselves, much longer than they liked.

The Third Voyage of Sinbad the Sailor

An extract from *The Arabian Nights Entertainments*,
retold by Andrew Lang

*Long ago, a Middle Eastern man called Sinbad went to sea to seek
his fortune in strange lands. On his first voyage, he landed on what
appeared to be an island, but was an enormous, sleeping whale! Sinbad
helped to save a king's horse from drowning and the king rewarded him
richly. On his second voyage, Sinbad found himself stranded in a valley
of diamonds. He was lifted out of the valley by a gigantic bird called a
roc, and returned to Baghdad with a fortune in gems.*

After a very short time the pleasant, easy
life I led made me quite forget the
perils of my two voyages. Moreover, as I was still in
the prime of life, it pleased me better to be up and
doing. So once more providing myself with the

rarest and choicest merchandise of Baghdad, I set sail with other merchants of my acquaintance for distant lands. We had touched at many ports and made much profit, when one day upon the open sea we were caught by a terrible wind. Lasting for several days, it finally drove us into harbour on a strange island.

"I would rather have come to anchor anywhere than here," exclaimed our captain. "This island is inhabited by hairy savages, who are certain to attack us. Whatever these dwarfs may do we dare not resist, since they swarm like locusts, and if one of them is killed the rest will fall upon us, and speedily make an end of us."

Only too soon we were to find out that the captain spoke truly. There appeared a vast multitude of hideous savages, not more than two feet high and covered with reddish fur. Throwing themselves into the waves, they surrounded our vessel. Chattering in a language we could not understand, and clutching at ropes and gangways, they swarmed up the ship's side with such speed and agility that they almost seemed to fly.

You may imagine the rage and terror that seized us as we watched, unable to do anything to stop them. They sailed our vessel to an island that lay a little further off, where they drove us ashore. Then they made off with our ship, leaving us helpless.

We wandered miserably inland, eating various herbs and fruits that we found as we went. Presently we saw in the distance what seemed to us to be a splendid palace, towards which we turned our weary steps. But when we reached it we saw that it was a castle, lofty, and strongly built. Pushing back the heavy, ebony doors we entered the courtyard, but upon the threshold of the great hall beyond it we paused, frozen with horror, at the sight that greeted us. On one side lay a huge pile of bones – human bones – and on the other numberless spits for roasting! Overcome with terror, we sank trembling to the ground and lay there in despair.

The sun was setting when a loud noise aroused

us. The door of the hall was violently burst open
and a horrible giant entered. He was as tall as a
palm tree and had one eye, which flamed like a
burning coal in the middle of his forehead. His
teeth were long and sharp, while his lower lip hung
down upon his chest. He had ears like an elephant's
ears, which covered his shoulders, and huge nails.

The giant examined us with his fearful eye, then
came towards us, and grabbed me by the back of the
neck, turning me this way and that. Feeling that I
was mere skin and bone he
set me down again and
went on to the next,
whom he treated in
the same fashion. At
last he came to the
captain, and
finding him the
fattest, he stuck
him upon a spit
and kindled a

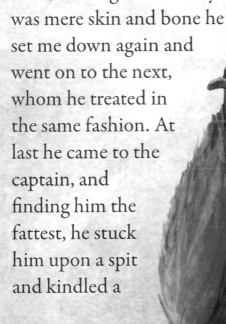

huge fire at which he roasted him. After the giant had supped he lay down to sleep, snoring like the loudest thunder. We lay shivering with horror the whole night through.

When day broke he awoke and went out. We bemoaned our horrible fate, until the hall echoed with our despairing cries. Though we were many and our enemy was alone, no plan could we devise to escape from the island. So at last, submitting to our sad fate, we spent the day in wandering up and down the island eating what we could find. When night came we returned to the castle, having sought in vain for any other place of shelter.

At sunset the giant returned, supped upon one of our unhappy comrades, slept and snored till dawn, and then left us as before. Our condition seemed to us so frightful that several of my companions thought it would be better to leap from the cliffs and perish in the waves at once, rather than await so miserable an end. But at last I had an idea to combat the giant. I told it to my companions, then added, "Plenty of driftwood lies along the shore. Let us make several rafts. If our plot succeeds, we can wait patiently for some passing ship to rescue us. If it fails, we must quickly take to our rafts. Frail as they are, we have more chance of saving our lives with them than we have if we remain here."

All agreed with me, and we spent the day building rafts, each capable of carrying three men. At nightfall we returned to the castle, and very soon in came the giant, and one more of our number was taken. But the time of our vengeance was at hand! As soon as he had finished his horrible repast he lay down to sleep as before, and when we heard him begin to snore I, and nine of the boldest of my comrades, rose softly and took a spit, which we made red-hot in the fire. Then we plunged it into the giant's eye, completely blinding him. Uttering a terrible cry, he sprang to his feet clutching in all directions to try to seize one of us. But we had all fled different ways as soon as the deed was done, and thrown ourselves flat upon the ground in corners where he was not likely to touch us.

After a vain search he fumbled about till he found the door, and fled out of it howling frightfully. We too fled from the castle and, stationing ourselves beside our rafts, waited to see what would happen.

Morning light showed our enemy approaching us, supported on either hand by two giants nearly as large and fearful as himself, while a crowd of others followed close upon their heels. Hesitating no longer we clambered upon our rafts and rowed with all our might out to sea. The giants seized up huge pieces of rock and, wading into the water, hurled them after us with such good aim that all the rafts except the one I was upon were swamped, and their luckless crews drowned. Indeed I and my two companions had all we could do to keep our own raft beyond the reach of the giants. But through hard rowing we at last reached the open sea.

The History of Jack the Giant-Killer

From Andrew Lang's *Blue Fairy Book*

*I*n the reign of the famous King Arthur there lived in Cornwall a lad named Jack, who was a boy of a bold temper. He took delight in hearing or reading of conjurers, giants and fairies, and used to listen eagerly to the deeds of the knights of King Arthur's Round Table.

In those days there lived on St Michael's Mount, off Cornwall, a huge giant, eighteen metres high and nine metres round. His fierce and savage looks were the terror of all who beheld him.

He dwelled in a gloomy cavern on the top of the

mountain, and used to wade over to the mainland in search of prey. He would throw oxen upon his back, and tie sheep and hogs round his waist, and march back to his abode.

The giant had done this for many years when Jack resolved to destroy him. Jack took a horn, a shovel, a pickaxe, his armour and a dark lantern, and one winter's evening he went to the mount. There he dug a pit twenty-two metres deep and twenty broad. He covered the top over so as to make it look like solid ground. Jack then blew his horn so loudly that the giant awoke and came out of his den, crying out, "You villain! You shall pay for this!" He had just finished, when, taking one step further, he tumbled into the pit, and Jack struck him a blow on the head with his pickaxe, which killed him. Jack then returned home to cheer his friends with the news.

Another giant, called Blunderbore, vowed to be revenged on Jack if ever he should have him in his power. This giant lived in an enchanted castle in a lonely wood and one day came across Jack lying under a tree in the wood, asleep. The giant carried Jack off to his castle, where he locked him up in a large room, the floor of which was covered with skulls and bones.

Soon afterwards the giant went to fetch his brother. Jack saw with terror through the bars of his prison the two giants approaching. Then he noticed in one corner of the room a strong rope. He made a slip knot at each end, and threw them over their heads, and tied it to the window bars. Then he pulled till they fell lifeless to the floor.

Jack next took a great bunch of keys from the pocket of Blunderbore, and went into the castle again. He searched through all the rooms, and in one of them found three ladies tied up. They told him that their husbands had been killed by the giants, who had then condemned them to be starved to death.

"Ladies," said Jack, "I have put an end to the monster and his wicked brother. I give you this castle and all the riches it contains, to make some amends for the dreadful pains you have felt." He then very politely gave them the keys of the castle.

Having hitherto been successful in all his undertakings, Jack resolved not to be idle in future. He furnished himself with a horse, a cap of knowledge, a sword of sharpness, shoes of swiftness and an invisible coat to help him carry out the tasks that lay before him.

He travelled over hills and dales till, arriving at the foot of a high mountain, he knocked at the door of a house. An old man let him in, and then said to Jack, "My son, on the top of this mountain is an enchanted castle, kept by the giant Galligantus and a vile magician. They seized a duke's daughter as she was walking in her father's garden, and then they brought her here transformed into a deer."

Jack promised that in the morning, at the risk of his life, he would break the enchantment. And after a sound sleep he rose early, put on his invisible coat, and got ready for the attempt.

When he had climbed to the top of the mountain he saw two fiery griffins, but he passed between them without the least fear of danger, for they could not see him because of his invisible coat. On the castle gate he found a golden trumpet, under which were written these lines:

Whoever can this trumpet blow
Shall cause the giant's overthrow.

As soon as Jack had read this he seized the trumpet and blew a shrill blast, which made the gates fly open and the very castle itself tremble.

The giant and the magician now knew that their wicked work was at an end, and they stood biting their thumbs and shaking with fear. Jack, with his sword of sharpness, soon killed the giant, and the magician was then carried away by a whirlwind.

Then every knight and beautiful lady who had been changed into birds and beasts returned to their proper shapes. The castle vanished away like smoke, and the head of the giant Galligantus was then sent to King Arthur.

The knights and ladies rested that night at the old man's house, and next day they set out for the Court. Jack's fame had now spread through the whole country, and the duke gave him his daughter in marriage. After this the king gave him a large estate, on which he and his lady lived the rest of their days in joy and contentment.

Tamlane

From *More English Fairy Tales*
by Joseph Jacobs

Young Tamlane was the son of Earl Murray, and Burd Janet was the daughter of Dunbar, Earl of March. And when they were young they loved one another and were betrothed to be married. But when the time came near for their marrying, Tamlane disappeared, and none knew what had become of him.

Many, many days after he had disappeared, Burd Janet was wandering in Carterhaugh Wood, though she had been warned not to go there. She came to a broom bush and began plucking it. She had not taken more than three flowers when by her side up started young Tamlane.

"Where have you come from, Tamlane?" Burd Janet said. "And why have you been away so long?"

"From Elfland I come," said young Tamlane. "The Queen of Elfland has made me her knight."

"But how did you get there?" asked Burd Janet.

"I was hunting one day, and as I rode anti-clockwise round a hill, a deep drowsiness fell upon me, and when I awoke, behold! I was in Elfland."

"Oh, tell me if aught I can do will save you?"

"Tomorrow night is Hallowe'en, and the fairy court will then ride through England and Scotland, and if you would rescue me from Elfland you must stand by Miles Cross between twelve and one o' the night, and cast holy water all around you."

"But how shall I know you," cried Burd Janet, "amid so many knights I've never seen before?"

"Let the first court of elves that come by pass. The next court you shall curtsey to, but do naught nor say aught. But the third court that comes by is the chief court, and at the head rides the Queen of Elfland. And I shall ride by her side upon a milk-white steed with a star in my crown. Watch my hands, Janet, the right one will be gloved but the left one will be bare, and by that token you will know me."

"But how do I save you?" asked Burd Janet.

"You must spring upon me suddenly, and I will fall to the ground. Then seize me quick, and whatever change befall me, for they will exercise all their magic on me, cling on till they turn me into red-hot iron. Then cast me into the water and I will be turned back into a man. Then cast your green mantle over me, and I shall be yours, and be part of the world again."

So Burd Janet promised to do all of this for Tamlane, and the next night at midnight she took her stand by Miles Cross and cast holy water all around her.

Soon there came riding by the Elfin Court, first over the mound went a troop on black steeds, and then another troop on brown. But in the third court, all on milk-white steeds, she saw the Queen of Elfland, and by her side a knight with a star in his crown, with his right hand gloved and the left bare. Then she knew this was Tamlane, and springing forward she seized the bridle of the milk-white steed and pulled its rider down. As soon as he had touched the ground she let go of the bridle and seized Tamlane in her arms.

"He's won, he's won amongst us all," shrieked out the eldritch crew, and they all came around her and tried their spells on young Tamlane.

First they turned him like frozen ice in Janet's arms, then into a huge flame of roaring fire. Then again, the fire vanished and an adder was skipping through her arms, but still Janet held on. And then they turned him into a snake that reared up as if to bite her, and yet she held on. Then suddenly a dove was struggling in her arms, and almost flew away. Then they turned him into a swan. At last he was turned into red-hot iron, and this Janet cast into a well of water, and then he turned back into a man. She quickly cast her green mantle over him, and young Tamlane was Burd Janet's. And the Elfin Court rode away, and Burd Janet and young Tamlane went their way homewards and were married soon afterwards.

The Twelve Brothers

Retold by Andrew Lang in his *Red Fairy Book*,
after the Brothers Grimm

There were once upon a time a king and a queen who had twelve children, all of whom were boys. One day the king said to his wife, "If our thirteenth child is a girl, all her twelve brothers must die, so that the kingdom may be hers alone."

Then he ordered twelve coffins to be made, and put these away in an empty room. Giving the key to his wife, he bade her tell no one of it.

The queen grieved and refused to be comforted, so much so that the youngest boy, who was always with her, and whom she had christened Benjamin, said to her one day, "Dear Mother, what makes you so sad?"

"My child," she answered, "I cannot tell you."

But Benjamin left her no peace, till she went and unlocked the room, and showed him the twelve little coffins and explained. She wept bitterly, but

her son comforted her and said, "Don't cry, dear Mother. We'll escape somehow."

"Yes," replied his mother, "that is what you must do – go with your eleven brothers out into the wood. Let one of you always sit on the highest tree you can find, keeping watch on the tower of the castle. If I give birth to a little son I will wave a white flag, and then you may safely return. But if I give birth to a little daughter I will wave a red flag, which will warn you to fly away as quickly as you can. Every night I will get up and pray for you."

Then she blessed her sons and they set out into the wood. They found a very high oak tree, and there they sat, turn about, keeping their eyes always fixed on the castle tower.

On the twelfth day, when the turn came to Benjamin, he noticed a flag waving in the air, but alas! It was not white, but blood red, the sign that told them they must all die. When the brothers heard this they were very angry, and said, "Shall we suffer death for the sake of a wretched girl? Let us vow to never befriend one of her sex."

Then they went their way deeper into the wood,

and in the middle of it, where it was thickest and darkest, they came upon a little enchanted house that stood empty.

"Let's live here," they said, "and you, Benjamin, you shall stay at home and keep house for us. We will go out and fetch food." So they went forth into the wood, and foraged and hunted. They lived for ten years in this little house, and the time slipped merrily away.

Meantime, their little sister grew up kind-hearted and of a fair countenance, with a gold star right in the middle of her forehead.

One day the girl looked down from her window and saw twelve boy's shirts hanging on the washing line to dry, and she asked her mother, "Who do these shirts belong to? Surely they are far too small for my father?"

And the queen answered sadly, "Dear child, they belong to your twelve brothers."

"But where are my twelve brothers?" said the girl. "I have never even heard of them."

"Heaven alone knows!" replied her mother. Then she took the girl and opened the locked-up room, and showed her the twelve coffins.

The queen told all that had happened, and when she had finished her daughter said, "Do not cry, dearest Mother. I will go and seek my brothers."

So the princess took the twelve shirts and went into the middle of the big wood. She walked all day long, and came in the evening to the little enchanted house.

She stepped in and found a youth who, marvelling at her beauty, at the royal robes she wore, and at the golden star on her forehead, asked her where she came from and where she was going.

"I am a princess," the girl answered, "and am seeking my twelve brothers. I mean to wander as far as the blue sky stretches over the earth till I find them."

Then she showed him the twelve shirts that she had taken with her, and Benjamin saw that it must be his sister, and said, "I am your youngest brother."

So they wept for joy and hugged each other.

After a time Benjamin said, "Dear sister, there is still a problem, for we had all agreed that we would never befriend any girl, because it was for the sake of a girl that we had to leave our kingdom. Go and hide till our eleven brothers come in, and I'll make matters right with them."

The princess did as she was bid, and soon the eleven brothers came home from hunting and sat down to supper.

"Well, well," Benjamin said to his brothers, "you've been out in the wood all the day and I've stayed quietly at home, and yet I've got the most exciting news!"

"Then tell us," they cried.

But he answered, "Only on one condition – that you promise not to be angry that I have befriended a girl."

"We shall not be angry," they promised, "only tell us the news."

Then Benjamin said, "Our sister is here!" and the

princess stepped forward, with her royal robes and with the golden star on her forehead, looking so lovely and sweet and charming that they all loved her on the spot.

They arranged that she should stay at home with Benjamin and help him in the housework, while the rest of the brothers went out into the wood to forage and hunt. The princess made herself so generally useful that her brothers were delighted, and they all lived happily together.

One day the two at home prepared a fine feast, and when they were all assembled they sat down and ate and drank and made merry.

Now there was a little garden round the enchanted house, in which grew twelve tall lilies. The girl, wishing to please her brothers, started to pluck the twelve flowers, meaning to present one to each of them after supper. But hardly had she begun when her brothers were turned into twelve ravens, who flew cawing over the wood, and the house and garden vanished also.

So the poor girl found herself left all alone in the wood, and as she looked round her she noticed an old woman standing close by, who said, "My child, what have you done? Why didn't you leave the flowers alone? Now your brothers are changed forever into ravens."

The girl asked, sobbing, "Is there no means of setting them free?"

"There is only one way," said the old woman, "and that is so difficult that you won't free them by it, for you would have to be dumb and not laugh for seven years, and if you spoke a single word it would slay your brothers."

Then the girl said to herself, "If that is all, I am quite sure I can free my brothers." So she searched for a high tree, and climbed up it and spun all day long, never laughing nor speaking one word.

Now it happened one day that a king who was out hunting had a greyhound, who ran sniffing to the tree on which the girl sat, and jumped round it, yelping and barking furiously. When the king looked up and beheld the beautiful princess with the golden star on her forehead, he was so enchanted that he asked her to be his wife. She gave no answer, but nodded slightly. Then the king climbed up the tree, lifted the princess down, and bore her home to his palace.

The marriage was celebrated with much ceremony, but the bride neither spoke nor laughed.

When they had lived a few years happily together, the king's mother, who was a wicked old woman, began to speak ill of the young queen, accusing her of many evil things. Of course, the queen could not speak for herself to protest, and eventually the king let himself be talked over, and condemned his wife to death.

So a great fire was lit in the courtyard of the palace, where she was to be burned, and the king watched from an upper window, crying bitterly, for he still loved his wife dearly. But just as she had been bound to the stake, and the flames were licking her garments, the very last moment of the seven years came. Then a sudden rushing sound was heard and twelve ravens swooped downwards. As soon as they touched the ground they turned into the queen's twelve brothers, and she knew that she had freed them. They quenched the flames and, unbinding their dear sister from the stake, they kissed and hugged her again and again. And now that she was able to speak, she told the king why she had been dumb and not able to laugh.

The king rejoiced greatly when he heard she was innocent, and they all lived happily ever after.

MONSTERS AND MISCHIEF

Tom Tit Tot

A Rumpelstiltskin story,
retold by Joseph Jacobs in *English Fairy Tales*

Once upon a time there was a woman who baked five pies. When they came out of the oven, they were that overbaked the crusts were too hard to eat. So she says to her daughter, "Darter, put you them there pies on the shelf, and leave 'em there a little, and they'll come again." She meant, you know, the crust would get soft.

But the girl, she says to herself, "Well, if they'll come again, I'll eat 'em now." And she set to work and ate 'em all, first and last.

Come suppertime the woman said, "Go you, and

get one o' them there pies. I dare say they've come again now."

The girl went and she looked, and there was nothing but the dishes. So back she came, and says she, "Noo, they ain't come again."

"Not one of 'em?" says the mother.

"Not one of 'em," says she.

"Well, come again, or not come again," said the woman, "I'll have one for supper."

"But you can't, if they ain't come," said the girl.

"But I can," says she. "Go you, and bring the best of 'em."

"Best or worst," says the girl, "I've ate 'em all, and you can't have one till that's come again."

Well, the woman she was done, and she took her spinning to the door, and as she span she sang,

"My darter ha' ate five, five pies today.

My darter ha' ate five, five pies today."

The king was coming down the street, and he heard her sing, but what she sang he couldn't hear, so he stopped and said, "What was that you were singing, my good woman?"

The woman was ashamed to let him hear what her daughter had been doing, so she started to sing, instead of that,

"My darter ha' spun five, five skeins today.

My darter ha' spun five, five skeins today."

"Stars o' mine!" said the king, "I never heard tell of anyone that could do that."

Then he said, "Look you here, I want a wife, and I'll marry your daughter. But look you here," says he, "eleven months out of the year she shall have all she likes to eat, and all the gowns she likes to get, and all the company she likes to keep. But the last month of the year she'll have to spin five skeins every day, and if she don't, I shall kill her."

"All right," says the woman, for she thought what a grand marriage that was. And as for the five skeins, when the time came, there'd be plenty of ways of getting out of it, and likeliest, he'd have forgotten all about it.

So they were married. And for eleven months the

girl had all she liked to eat, and all the gowns she liked to get, and all the company she liked to keep.

But when the time was getting over, she began to think about the skeins and to wonder if he had 'em in mind. But not one word did he say about 'em, and she thought he'd wholly forgotten 'em.

However, on the last day of the last month the king takes her to a room she'd never set eyes on before. There was nothing in it but a spinning wheel and a stool. And says he, "Now, my dear, you'll be shut in here tomorrow with some victuals and some flax, and if you haven't spun five skeins by the night, your head will go off." And away the king went about his business.

Well, she was that frightened. She'd always been such a careless girl that she didn't so much as know how to spin, and what was she to do tomorrow with no one to come to help her? She sat down on a stool in the kitchen, and lord, how she did cry!

However, all of a sudden she heard a sort of knocking low down on the door. She upped and opened it. And what should she see but a little black imp with a long tail, that looked up at her right curious and said, "What are you a-crying for?"

"What's that to you?" says she.

"Never you mind," it said, "but tell me what you're a-crying for."

"That won't do me no good if I do," says she.

"You don't know that," it said, and twirled its tail round.

"Well," says she, "that won't do no harm, if that don't do no good," and she upped and told about the pies, and the skeins, and everything.

"This is what I'll do," says the little black imp, "I'll come to your window every morning and take the flax and bring it spun at night."

"What's your pay?" says she.

The imp looked out the corner of its eyes, and said, "I'll give you three chances every night to guess my name, and if you haven't guessed it before the month's up, you shall be mine."

Well, she thought she'd be sure to guess the imp's name before the month was up. "All right," says she, "I agree."

"All right," it says, and lord, how it twirled its tail round and round!

Well, the next day, her husband took her into the room, and there was the flax and the day's food. "Now there's the flax," says he, "and if that ain't spun up this night, off goes your head." And then he went out and locked the door.

He'd hardly gone, when there was a knocking against the window. She upped and she opened it, and there sure enough was the little black imp sitting on the ledge.

"Where's the flax?" says he.

"Here it be," says she, and she gave it to him.

Well, come the evening a knocking came again to the window. She upped and she opened it, and there was the little black imp with five skeins of flax on his arm. "Here it be," says he, and he gave it to her. "Now, what's my name?"

"What, is it Bill?" says she.

"Noo, that ain't," says he, and he twirled his tail.

"Is it Ned?" says she.

"Noo, it ain't," says he, and he twirled his tail.

"Well, is it Mark?" says she.

"Noo, it ain't," says he, and he twirled his tail harder, and away he flew.

When her husband came in, there were the five skeins ready for him. "I see I shan't have to kill you tonight, my dear," says he. "You'll have your food and your flax in the morning," and away he goes.

Well every day the flax and the food were brought, and every day that there little black imp used to come mornings and evenings. And all the day the girl sat trying to think of names to say to it when it came at night. But she never hit on the right one.

And as it got towards the end of the month, the little black imp began to look so maliceful, and it twirled its tail faster and faster each time she gave a guess.

At last it came to the last day but one. The little black imp came at night along with the five skeins, and said,

"What, ain't you got my name yet?"

"Is it Nicodemus?" says she.

"Noo, 'tain't," he says.

"Is it Sam?" says she.

"Noo, 'tain't," he says.

"A-well, is it Methusalem?" says she.

"Noo, 'tain't that neither," he says.

Then the little imp looks at her with its eyes like a coal o' fire, and says, "Woman, there's only tomorrow night, and then you'll be mine!" And away it flew.

Well, she felt horrid. However, she heard the king coming along the passage.

In he came, and when he sees the five skeins, he says, "Well, my dear, I don't see but what you'll have your skeins ready tomorrow night as well, and as I reckon I shan't have to kill you, I'll have supper in here tonight." So they brought supper, and another stool for him, and down the two sat.

Well, he hadn't eaten but a mouthful or so, when he stops and begins to laugh.

"What is it?" says she.

"A-why," says he, "I was out a-hunting today, and I got away to a place in the wood I'd never seen before. And there was an old chalk pit. And I heard a sort of humming. So I got off my horse, and I went right quiet to the pit, and I looked down. Well, what should there be but the funniest little black imp you ever set eyes on. And what was it doing but it had a spinning wheel, and it was spinning wonderful fast, and twirling its tail. And as it span it sang,

    'Nimmy nimmy not
    My name's Tom Tit Tot.'"

Well, when the girl heard this, she felt as if she could have jumped out her skin for joy, but she didn't say a word.

Next day that there little black imp looked so maliceful when it came for the flax. And when night came, she heard it knocking against the window panes. She opened the window, and the imp came right in on the ledge. It was grinning from ear to ear, and ooh, its tail was twirling round so fast!

"What's my name?" it says.

"Is it Solomon?" she says.

"Noo, 'tain't," it says, and it started to come into the room.

"Well, is that Zebedee?" says she again.

"Noo, 'tain't," says the imp. And then it laughed and twirled its tail till you couldn't hardly see it.

"Take time, woman," it says, "next guess, and you're mine." And the imp stretched out its little hands at her.

Well, she backed a step or two, and she looked at

it, and then she laughed out, and says she, pointing her finger at it,

    "Nimmy nimmy not

     Your name's Tom Tit Tot."

    Well, when it heard her, the imp gave an awful shriek and away it flew into the dark, and she never saw it any more.

Buchettino

By Thomas Frederick Crane

Once upon a time there was a child whose name was Buchettino. One morning his mamma called him and said, "Buchettino, will you do me a favour? Go and sweep the stairs." Buchettino, who was very obedient, did not wait to be told a second time, but went at once to sweep the stairs.

After sweeping all around, he found a penny. Then he said to himself, "What shall I do with this penny? I have half a mind to buy some dates... but no! For I should have to throw away the stones. I will buy some apples... no! I will not, for I should have to throw away the core. I will buy some nuts… but no! For I should have to throw away the shells. What shall I buy, then? I will buy – I will buy – enough! I will buy a pennyworth of figs."

No sooner said than done. Buchettino bought a pennyworth of figs and went and sat up in a tree to eat them. While he was eating, an ogre passed by. Seeing Buchettino eating figs in the tree, the ogre said, "Buchettino, my dear Buchettino, give me a little fig with your dear little hand. If you don't, I will eat you!"

Buchettino threw the ogre a fig, but it fell in the dirt. The ogre repeated, "Buchettino, my dear Buchettino, give me a little fig with your dear little hand. If you don't, I will eat you!"

Then Buchettino threw him another, which also fell in the dirt. The ogre said again, "Buchettino, my dear Buchettino, give me a little fig with your dear little hand. If you don't, I will eat you!"

Poor Buchettino. He did not see the trick and did not know that the ogre was trying to get him into his bag and eat him up. What does Buchettino do? He leans down and foolishly gives the ogre a fig with his little hand.

The ogre, who wanted nothing better, suddenly grabbed Buchettino by the arm and put him into his bag. Then he put the bag on his back and headed for his home, crying, "Wife, my wife, put the kettle on the fire, for I have caught Buchettino! Wife, my wife, put the kettle on the fire, for I have caught Buchettino!"

When the ogre was near his house he put the bag on the

ground and went off to attend to something else. Buchettino, with a knife that he had in his pocket, cut the bag open in a moment, filled it with large stones and then said, "My legs, run away for we need to go."

When the rascal of an ogre returned he picked up the bag and scarcely had he arrived home when he said to his wife, "Tell me, my wife, have you put the kettle on the fire?" She answered at once, "Yes." "Then," said the ogre, "we will cook Buchettino. Come here and help me." Taking the bag, they carried it to the hearth to throw poor Buchettino into the kettle, but instead they found only the stones. Imagine how cheated the ogre felt. He was so angry that he bit his hands. The ogre could not bear the thought of losing Buchettino, and he swore to find him again and get his revenge.

So the next day, the ogre began to go all about the city and to look in all the hiding places. At last he happened to raise his eyes and saw Buchettino on a balcony, laughing so hard that his mouth stretched from ear to ear. The ogre thought he should burst with rage, but he pretended not to be angry and in a very sweet tone he said, "Buchettino, tell me, how did you manage to climb up there?"

Buchettino answered, "Do you really want to know? Then listen. I put dishes upon dishes, glasses upon glasses, pans upon pans, kettles upon kettles. Afterwards I climbed up on them and here I am."

"Ah! Is that so?" said the stupid ogre. "Then wait a bit!" And quickly he took so many dishes, glasses, pans and kettles, and made a great mountain of them. Then he began to climb up to try and catch Buchettino. But when he was nearly on the top – *crash!* – everything fell down. That rascal of an ogre fell down on the stones and was cheated again. The ogre was so cross he went off to another country and never troubled Buchettino again.

Then Buchettino, very pleased with himself, ran home to his mamma.

The Prince
and the
Dragon

From Andrew Lang's *Crimson Fairy Book*

Once upon a time there lived an emperor who had three sons. They were all fine young men, who were very fond of hunting, and scarcely a day passed without one or other of them going out to look for game.

One morning the eldest mounted his horse and set out for a forest where wild animals of all sorts were to be found. He had not long left the castle, when a hare sprang out of a thicket and dashed across the road in front. The young man gave chase over hill and dale, till at last the hare took refuge in a mill by the side of a river. The prince followed and entered the mill, but stopped in terror by the door, for, instead of a hare, before him stood a dragon, breathing flames. At this fearful sight the prince turned to fly, but a fiery tongue coiled round his waist, and drew him into the dragon's mouth, and he was seen no more.

A week passed, and when the prince never came back everyone in the town began to grow uneasy. At last his next brother told the emperor that he likewise would go out to hunt, and that perhaps he would find some clue as to his brother's disappearance. Hardly had the castle gates closed than the hare sprang out of the bushes as before, and led the huntsman up hill and down dale, till they reached the mill. Into this the hare flew with the prince at his heels, when, lo! Instead of the hare, there stood a dragon breathing flames! And out shot a fiery tongue which coiled round the prince's waist and lifted him into the dragon's mouth, and he was seen no more.

Days went by, and the emperor waited for the sons who never came, and could not sleep at night for wondering what had become of them. His youngest son wished to go in search of his brothers, but for a long time the emperor refused to listen, lest he should lose him also. But the prince begged so hard, and promised so often that he would be very careful, that at length the emperor agreed.

Full of hope the young prince started on his way, but no sooner was he outside the city than a hare sprang out of the bushes and ran before him, till they reached the mill. As before, the animal dashed through the open door, but this time he was not followed by the prince. Wiser than his brothers, the young man turned away, saying, "There are as good hares in the forest as any that have come out of it, and when I have caught them, I can come back and look for you."

For many hours he rode up and down the mountain, but saw nothing, and at last he went back to the mill. Here he found an old woman sitting, whom he greeted pleasantly.

"Good morning to you, little mother," he said.

And the old woman answered, "Good morning, my son."

"Tell me, little mother," went on the prince, "where shall I find my hare?"

"My son," replied the old woman, "that was no hare, but a dragon who has led many men hither, and then has eaten them all."

At these words the prince's heart grew heavy, and he cried, "Then my brothers must have come here, and have been eaten!"

"You have guessed right," answered the old woman, "and you should go home at once, before the same fate overtakes you."

"Will you not come with me out of this dreadful place?" said the young man.

"He took me prisoner, too," answered she, "and I cannot shake off his chains."

"Then listen to me," cried the prince. "When the dragon comes back, ask him where he always goes when he leaves here, and what makes him so strong. And when you have coaxed the secret from him, tell me the next time I come."

So the prince went home, and the old woman remained at the mill, and as soon as the dragon returned she said to him, "Where have you been all this time?"

"I have travelled far," answered he.

Then the old woman began to flatter him and to praise his cleverness, and when she thought she had got him into a good temper, she said, "I have wondered so often where you get your strength from. I do wish you would tell me. I would stoop and kiss the place out of pure love!"

The dragon laughed at the old woman, and answered, "In the hearthstone yonder lies the secret of my strength."

Then the old woman jumped up and kissed the hearth, whereat the dragon laughed the more, and said, "You foolish creature! I was only jesting. It is not in the hearthstone, but in that tall tree that lies

the secret of my strength." Then the old woman jumped up again, put her arms round the tree and kissed it heartily. Loudly laughed the dragon when he saw what she was doing.

"Fool," he cried, "did you really believe that my strength came from that tree?"

"Where is it from then?" asked the old woman, rather crossly, for she did not like being made fun of.

"My strength," replied the dragon, "lies far away. So far that you could never reach it. Far, far from here is a kingdom, and by its capital city is a lake, and in the lake is a dragon, and inside the dragon is a wild boar, and inside the wild boar a hare, and inside the hare a pigeon, and

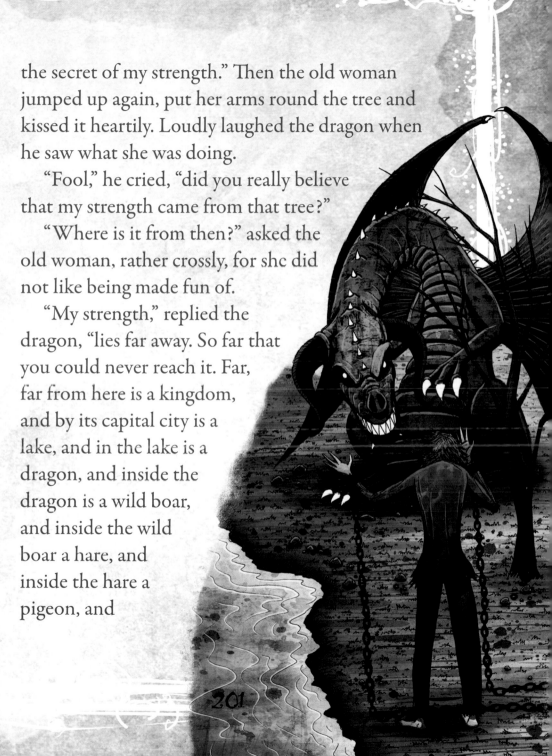

inside the pigeon a sparrow, and inside the sparrow is my strength." And when the old woman heard this, she thought it was no use flattering him any longer, for never, never, could she take his strength from him.

The following morning, when the dragon had left the mill, the prince came back, and the old woman told him everything that the creature had said. He listened in silence, and then returned to the castle, where he put on a suit of shepherd's clothes, and taking a staff in his hand, he went forth to seek a place as tender of sheep.

For some time he wandered from village to town, till he came to a large city in a distant kingdom, surrounded on three sides by a great lake, which happened to be the very lake in which the dragon lived. As was his custom, he stopped everybody whom he met in the streets that looked likely to want a shepherd and begged them to engage him, but no one needed one. The prince was beginning to lose heart, when a man said that he had better go and ask the emperor, as he was in search of someone to see after his flocks.

When the young man knelt before the emperor, His Majesty said, "Outside the city walls you will find a large lake, and by its banks lie the richest meadows in my kingdom. When you are leading out your flocks to pasture, they will run straight to these meadows, and none that have gone there have ever come back. Take heed, therefore, my son, not to suffer your sheep to go where they will, but drive them to any spot that you think best."

With a low bow the prince promised to do his best to keep the sheep safe. Then he went to the market place, where he bought two greyhounds, a hawk and a set of pipes. After that he took the sheep out to pasture. The instant the animals caught sight of the lake, they trotted off as fast as their legs would go to the green meadows round it. The prince did not try to stop them. He only placed his hawk on the branch of a tree, laid his pipes on the grass and bade the greyhounds sit still. Then, rolling up his sleeves and trousers, he waded into the water crying as he did so, "Dragon! If you are not a coward, come out and fight with me!"

And a voice answered from the depths of the lake, "I am waiting for you, O prince." And the dragon reared out of the water, huge and horrible to see.

The prince sprang upon him and they grappled with each other and fought together till the sun was high, and it was noon. Then the dragon gasped, "O prince, let me dip my burning head once into the lake, and I will hurl you up to the sky."

But the prince answered, "Oh ho, my good dragon, do not crow too soon! If the emperor's daughter were only here, and would kiss me on the forehead, I would throw you up higher still!" And suddenly the dragon's hold loosened and he fell back into the lake.

As soon as it was evening, the prince washed away all signs of the fight, took his hawk upon his shoulder, and his pipes under his arm, and with his

greyhounds in front and his flock following after him he set out for the city. As they passed through the streets the people stared in wonder, for never before had any flock returned from the lake.

The next morning he rose early and led his sheep down the road to the lake. This time, however, the emperor sent two men on horseback to ride behind him, with orders to watch without being seen. As soon as the sheep ran towards the meadows, they turned aside up a steep hill, which overhung the lake. When the shepherd reached the place he laid, as before, his pipes on the grass and bade the greyhounds sit beside them, while the hawk he perched on the branch of the tree. Then he rolled up his trousers and his sleeves, and waded into the water crying, "Dragon! If you are not a coward, come out and fight with me!"

And the dragon answered, "I am waiting for you, O prince," and he reared out of the water, huge and horrible to see. Again they clasped each other tight and fought till it was noon, and when the sun was at its hottest, the dragon gasped, "O prince, let me dip my burning head once in the lake, and I will hurl you up to the sky."

But the prince answered, "Oh ho, my good dragon, do not crow too soon! If the emperor's daughter were only here, and would kiss me on the forehead, I would throw you up higher still!" And suddenly the dragon's hold loosened and he fell back into the lake.

As soon as it was evening the prince again collected his sheep and, playing on his pipes, he marched before them into the city. And when he passed through the gates all the people came out of their houses to stare in wonder, because they had once more returned.

Meanwhile the two horsemen had ridden quickly back and told the emperor all. The emperor listened eagerly, then called his daughter to him and repeated it to her. "Tomorrow," he said, when he had finished, "you shall go with the shepherd to the lake, and you shall kiss him on the forehead."

But when the princess heard these words, she burst into tears and sobbed out, "Will you really send me, your only child, to that dreadful place, from which most likely I shall never come back?"

"Fear nothing, my little daughter, all will be well. Many shepherds have gone to that lake and none have ever returned. But this one has in these two days fought twice with the dragon and has escaped without a wound. So I hope tomorrow he will kill the dragon, and deliver this land from the monster who has slain so many of our bravest men."

Scarcely had the sun begun to peep over the hills next morning, when the princess stood by the shepherd's side, ready to go to the lake. He was brimming over with joy, but the princess only wept bitterly. "Dry your tears, I implore you," said he. "If you will do what I ask, and when the time comes, run and kiss my forehead, you have nothing to fear."

Merrily the shepherd blew on his pipes as he marched at the head of his flock, only stopping every now and then to say to the weeping girl at his side,

"Do not cry so. Trust me and fear nothing."

And so they reached the lake.

In an instant the sheep were scattered all over the meadows, and the prince placed his hawk on the tree, and his pipes on the grass, while he bade his greyhounds lie beside them. Then he rolled up his trousers and his sleeves, and waded into the water, calling, "Dragon! If you are not a coward, come forth, and let us have one more fight together."

And the dragon answered, "I am waiting for you, O prince," and reared out of the water, huge and horrible to see. Swiftly he drew near to the bank, and the prince sprang to meet him, and they grasped each other and fought till it was noon. And when the sun was at its hottest, the dragon cried, "O prince, let me dip my burning head in the lake, and I will hurl you to the sky."

But the prince answered, "Oh ho, my good dragon, do not crow too soon! If the emperor's daughter were only here, and she would kiss my forehead, I would throw you higher still."

Hardly had he spoken, when the princess, who had been listening, ran up and kissed him on the forehead. Then the prince swung the dragon straight up into the clouds, and when he touched the earth again, he broke into a thousand pieces. Out of the pieces there sprang a wild boar and it galloped away, but the prince called his hounds to give chase, and they caught the boar and killed it. Out of the pieces there sprang a hare, and in a moment the greyhounds were after it, and they caught it and killed it. Out of the hare there came a pigeon. Quickly the prince let loose his

hawk, which soared straight into the air, then swooped upon the bird and brought it to his master. The prince cut open its body and found the sparrow inside, just as the old woman had said.

"Now," cried the prince, holding the sparrow in his hand, "tell me where I can find my brothers."

"Do not hurt me," answered the sparrow, "and I will tell you with all my heart. Behind your father's castle stands a mill, and in the mill are three slender twigs. Cut off these twigs and strike their roots with them, and the iron door of a cellar will open. In the cellar you will find as many people, young and old, women and children, as would fill a kingdom, and among them are your brothers."

By this time twilight had fallen, so the prince washed in the lake, took the hawk on his shoulder and the pipes under his arm, and with his greyhounds before him and his flock behind him, marched gaily into the town, the princess following them all, still trembling with fright. And so they passed through the streets, thronged with a wondering crowd, till they reached the castle.

Unknown to anyone, the emperor had stolen out on horseback, and had hidden on the hill, where he could see all that happened. When all was over, and the power of the dragon was broken forever, he rode quickly back to the castle, and was ready to receive the prince with open arms, and to promise him his daughter as a wife.

The wedding took place with great splendour, and for a whole week the town was hung with coloured lamps, and tables were spread in the hall of the castle for all who chose to come and eat. And when the feast was over, the prince told the emperor and the people who he really was, and everyone rejoiced still more. Preparations were made for the prince and princess to return to their own kingdom, for the prince was impatient to set free his brothers.

The first thing he did when he reached his native country was to hasten to the mill, where he found the three twigs as the sparrow had told him. The moment that he struck their roots the iron door flew open, and from the cellar a countless multitude of men and women streamed forth. He bade them go one by one wheresoever they would, while he waited by the door till his brothers passed through. How delighted they were to meet again, and to hear all that the prince had done to deliver them. And they went home and served him all the days of their lives, for they said that only he was fit to be king.

The Buggane of the Church

By Sophia Morrison

A long time ago, some monks came to the broad, rough meadow that is between dark Greeba Mountain and the high road. They chose a nice place and set up a church on it. But they did not know about the power of the Buggane, who had his haunt in the mountain.

The Buggane was very angry and he said to himself, "I'll have no peace night or day with their jingling bells if I let them finish the building." And, as he had nothing else to do, he thought he would amuse himself by taking off the roof of the church.

So, when the roof of the church was first put on, a dreadful sound was heard that very night. When the people of Greeba got up early next morning, they found their church roofless, and planks and broken beams all around the place.

After a time and with great effort, the roof was put on again. But when it was on, a great storm arose in the night and it was blown down from the walls, exactly as before. This put fear in the people, for they were sure now that it was the evil Buggane himself that was doing the mischief. But, though they were terrified, they decided to make one more attempt, and the third roof was nearly finished.

Now, there was a brave little tailor living about a mile from Greeba. Because he did not have much money, he made a bet with a friend that when the new roof was on, he would not only spend the first night in the church, he would also make a pair of breeches there. The bet was taken up eagerly, as it was hoped that if the roof was up for one night, it would be left on.

So Tim – that was the name of the tailor – went to the church on the very first evening after the new roof had been put on. Tim took with him cloth, needle and thread, thimble and scissors. He entered the church boldly, lit a couple of big candles, and looked all over the building to see that everything was right. Then he locked the door so that there was no way to get in. He cut out the cloth and, seating himself cross-legged, he set to work at the breeches.

With a long thread and needle, Tim bent low over his work, his fingers moving backwards and forwards. The breeches had got to be finished or he would lose his bet, so he stitched away as fast as he could, thinking about the money the people would have to give him.

The tailor's courage rose high and he said to himself, "It's all foolishness about the Buggane."

But at that very minute the ground heaved under him and rumbling sounds came up from below. The sounds grew louder underneath and Tim glanced quickly up. All of a sudden, a great big head broke a hole through the stone floor just before the tailor, and came rising up slowly through the hole.

The head was covered with a mane of coarse, black hair. It had eyes like torches and glittering sharp tusks. When the head had risen above the stone floor, the fiery eyes glared fiercely at Tim. The big, ugly, red mouth opened wide, and a dreadful voice said, "You rascal, what business have you here?"

Tim paid no attention, but worked harder still at the breeches, for he knew he had no time to lose.

"Do you see this big head of mine?" yelled the Buggane loudly.

"I see, I see!" replied Tim, mockingly.

Up came a big, broad pair of shoulders, then a thick arm shot out and a great fist shook in the tailor's face.

"Do you see my long arms?" roared the terrible voice of the Buggane.

"I see, I see!" answered Tim, boldly.

The Buggane kept rising and rising up through the hole, until the horrible, ugly, hairy form, covered with wrinkles, had risen quite out of the hole in the ground.

"Do you see this big body of mine?" roared the Buggane, angry that Tim showed no fear of him.

"I see, I see!" replied the tailor, while at the same time stitching with all his might at the breeches.

"Do you see my sharp claws?" roared the Buggane in a more angry voice than before.

"I see, I see!" answered the tailor again, without raising his eyes and continuing to pull the thread with all his might.

"Do you see my large foot?"

thundered the Buggane, drawing up one big foot and putting it down on the stone floor with a thud that made the walls shake.

"I see, I see!" replied the tailor as before, stitching hard at the breeches and starting to take long stitches.

Lifting up his other foot, the terrible Buggane, in a furious rage, yelled, "Do you see my rough arms, my bony fingers, my hard fists, my—?"

Before the Buggane could utter another word or pull his other foot out of the ground, the tailor quickly jumped up and made two stitches together. The breeches were at last finished, so then with one large spring the tailor made a leap through the nearest window.

But scarcely was he outside the walls of the church, when down fell the new roof with a terrible crash, which made the tailor run a great deal more nimbly than he had ever run before.

Hearing the Buggane's fiendish guffaws of laughter behind him, he took to his heels and sped along Douglas Road, the breeches under his arms and the furious Buggane in full chase.

The tailor made for Marown Church, which was only a little distance away, and he knew he would be safe if he could only reach the churchyard.

Tim ran faster still, reached the wall, leapt over it like a hunted hare, and fell wearily upon the grass. He was under the shadow of the church, where the Buggane did not have the power to follow him.

So furious was the monster at this that he seized his own head with his two hands, tore it off his body and sent it flying over the wall after the tailor. The head burst at the tailor's feet with a terrific explosion. With that, the Buggane vanished and was never seen or heard of again. The tailor was not hurt and he won the bet, for no one grumbled at the few long stitches put into the breeches.

And as for the church, its roof was never replaced. It stands in the green meadow under the shadow of rocky Greeba Mountain, and there its grey, roofless ruins are to be found now.

Mr Miacca

From *English Fairy Tales*
by Joseph Jacobs

Tommy Grimes was sometimes good, and sometimes bad. Now his mother used to say to him, "Tommy, Tommy, be good, and don't go out into the street, or else Mr Miacca will take you."

But one day when he was bad he went out into the street and, sure enough, Mr Miacca did catch him and popped him into a bag, and took him off to his house.

Mr Miacca pulled Tommy out of the bag and set him down, and felt his arms and legs. "You're rather tough," says he, "but you're all I've got for supper, and you'll not taste bad boiled. But I've forgot the herbs, and it's bitter you'll taste without herbs." And he called Mrs Miacca.

Mrs Miacca came out of another room and said, "What d'ye want, my dear?"

"Here's a little boy for supper, but I've forgot the herbs. Mind him, while I go for them," he replied.

"All right, my love," says Mrs Miacca, and off her husband goes.

Then Tommy Grimes said to Mrs Miacca, "Does Mr Miacca always have little boys for supper?"

"Mostly, my dear," said Mrs Miacca, "if little boys are bad enough, and get in his way."

"Don't you have anything else? No pudding?" asked Tommy.

"Ah, I loves pudding," says Mrs Miacca. "But it's not often the likes of me gets pudding."

"Why, my mother is making a pudding this very day," said Tommy Grimes, "and I am sure she'd give you some, if I ask her. Shall I run and get some?"

"Now, that's a thoughtful boy," said Mrs Miacca, "only don't be long and be back for supper."

So off Tommy pelters, and right glad he was to get off so cheap.

For many a long day he was as good as good could be, and never went out into the street. But he couldn't always be good. One day he went out into the street, and as luck would have it, he hadn't scarcely gone out when Mr Miacca grabbed him up, popped him in his bag, and took him home.

When he got him there, Mr Miacca dropped him out, and when he saw him, he said, "Ah, you're the youngster what served me and my missus that shabby trick, leaving us without any supper. Well, you shan't do it again. I'll watch over you myself. Here, get under the sofa, and I'll sit on it and wait for the pot to boil for you."

So poor Tommy Grimes had to creep under the sofa, and Mr Miacca sat on it. And they waited, and they waited, but still the pot didn't boil. At last Mr Miacca got tired of waiting, and he said, "Here, I'm not going to wait any longer. Put out your leg, and I'll stop your giving us the slip."

But Tommy put out a leg of the sofa. Mr Miacca chopped it off and popped it in the pot.

Suddenly he called for his wife, but nobody answered. So he went into the next room to look for Mrs Miacca. While he was there, Tommy crept out from under the sofa and ran out of the door.

So Tommy Grimes ran home, and he never went out into the street again until he was old enough to go alone.

The Story of the Fisherman

From *The Arabian Nights Entertainments*,
retold by Andrew Lang

There was, once upon a time, a fisherman so old and poor that he could scarcely manage to support his wife and children. He went to fish very early every day. One morning, he started out by moonlight. He threw his nets and as he was drawing them in he felt a great weight. The fisherman thought he had caught a large fish, and he felt very pleased. But a moment afterwards, seeing that he had in his nets only the carcass of an ass, he was much disappointed.

Vexed, the fisherman threw his nets in a second

time. In drawing them in he again felt a great weight, so that he thought they were full of fish. But he found only a large basket full of rubbish. He was much annoyed. "O Fortune," he cried, "do not trifle thus with me, a poor fisherman, who can hardly support his family!"

So saying, he threw his nets in for the third time. But he only drew in stones, shells and mud. He was almost in despair.

Then he threw his nets for the fourth time. When he thought he had a fish he drew them in with a great deal of trouble. There was no fish, but he found a yellow vase, which by its weight seemed full of something, and he noticed that it was fastened and sealed with lead, with the impression of a seal. The fisherman was delighted. "I will sell it," he said, "and with the money I shall get for it I shall buy a measure of wheat."

He examined the vase on all sides and shook it to see if it would rattle. But he heard nothing, and so, judging from the impression of the seal and the lid, he thought there must be something precious inside. To find out, he took his knife, and with a little trouble he opened it. He turned it upside down, but nothing came out, which surprised him very much. He set it in front of him, and while he was looking at it attentively, such a thick smoke came out that he had to step back a pace or two. This smoke rose up to the clouds and, stretching over the sea and the shore, formed a thick mist, which caused the fisherman much astonishment. When all the smoke was out of the vase it gathered itself together, and became a thick mass in which appeared a genie, twice as large as the largest giant. When he saw such a terrible-looking monster, the fisherman would liked to have run away, but he trembled

so with fright that he could not move a step.

"Great king of the genies," cried the large monster, "I will never again disobey you!"

And at these words the fisherman took courage.

"What is this you are saying, genie? Tell me how you came to be shut up in that vase."

At this, the genie looked at the fisherman haughtily. "Speak to me more civilly," he said, "before I kill you."

"Alas! Why should you kill me?" cried the fisherman. "I have just freed you. Have you already forgotten that?"

"No," answered the genie, "but that will not prevent me from killing you. And I am only going to grant you one favour, and that is to choose the manner of your death."

"What have I done to you?" asked the fisherman.

"I cannot treat you in any other way," said the genie, "and if you would know why, listen to my story. I rebelled against the king of the genies. To punish me, he shut me up in this vase of copper, and he put on the leaden seal, which is enchantment enough to prevent my coming out. Then he had the vase thrown into the sea. During the first period of my captivity I vowed that if anyone should free me before a hundred years were passed, I would make him rich even after his death. But that century passed, and no one freed me. In the second century I vowed that I would give all the treasures in the world to my deliverer, but he never came. In the third, I promised to make him a king, to be always near him, and to grant him three wishes every day, but that century passed away as the other two had done, and I remained in the same plight. At last I grew angry at being captive for so long, and I vowed that if anyone would release me I would kill him at once, and would only allow him to choose in what manner he should die. So you see, as you have freed me today, choose in what way you will die."

The fisherman was very unhappy. "What an unlucky man I am to have freed you! I implore you to spare my life."

"I have told you," said the genie, "that it is impossible. Choose quickly, you are wasting time."

The fisherman began to devise a plot.

"Since I must die," he said, "before I choose the manner of my death, I conjure you on your honour to tell me if you really were in that vase?"

"Yes, I was," answered the genie.

"I really cannot believe it," said the fisherman. "That vase could not contain one of your feet even, and how could your whole body go in? I cannot believe it unless I see you do it."

Then the genie began to change himself into smoke, which, as before, spread over the sea and the shore, and which, then collecting itself together, began to go back into the vase slowly and evenly till there was nothing left outside. Then a voice came from the vase which said to the fisherman, "Well, unbelieving fisherman, here I am in the vase. Do you believe me now?"

The fisherman, instead of answering, took the lid of lead and shut it down quickly on the vase.

"Now, O genie," he cried, "ask pardon of me, and choose by what death you will die! But no, it will be better if I throw you into the sea whence I drew you out. And I will build a house on the shore to warn fishermen who come to cast their nets here, against fishing up such a wicked genie as you are, who vows to kill the man who frees you."

At these words the genie did all he could to get out, but he could not, because of the enchantment of the lid.

The Ogre of Rashomon

From *Japanese Fairy Tales*
by Yei Theodora Ozaki

*L*ong ago in Kyoto, the people of the city were terrified by, it was said, a dreadful ogre. He haunted the Gate of Rashomon at twilight and seized whoever passed by. It was whispered that the ogre was a horrible cannibal, who not only killed the unhappy victims but ate them also. Everybody in the town and neighbourhood was in great fear, and no one dared venture out after sunset near the Gate of Rashomon, for fear of the terrible stories.

Five valiant knights came travelling through the province. One night, as they sat at a feast, toasting each other's healths and exploits, the first knight, Hojo, said to the others, "Have you heard the rumours about the ogre at the Gate of Rashomon?"

The second knight, Watanabe, answered him, saying, "Do not talk such nonsense! There is no longer such thing as ogres."

"Then go there yourself and find out whether it is true or not," said Hojo.

Watanabe could not bear the thought that Hojo should believe he was afraid, so he got ready to go at once. He buckled on his long sword, put on a coat of armour and tied on his large helmet.

When he was ready to start he said to the others, "Give me something so that I can prove I have been there!" One of the men got a roll of writing paper and his box of Indian ink and brushes. Then the four men wrote their names on a piece of paper.

"I will take this," said Watanabe, "and put it on the Gate of Rashomon. So tomorrow morning you will all go and look at it. I may be able to catch an ogre or two by then!" And he mounted his horse and rode off gallantly.

It was a moonless and stormy night, but Watanabe sped on and at last he reached the Gate of Rashomon. Peer as he might through the darkness he could see no sign of an ogre.

"It is just as I thought," said Watanabe to himself. "There are certainly no ogres here. It is only an old woman's story. I will stick this paper on the gate so that the others can see I have been here when they come tomorrow, and then I will make my way home and laugh at them all."

He fastened the piece of paper, signed by his four companions, on the gate and then turned his horse's head towards home.

As he did so, his helmet was seized from the back. "Who are you?" cried Watanabe fearlessly. He then put out his hand and groped around to find out who or what it was that held him by the helmet. As he did so he touched something that felt like an arm – it was covered with hair and was as big as the trunk of a tree!

Watanabe knew at once that this was the arm of an ogre, so he drew his sword and cut at it fiercely. There

was a loud yell of pain, and then the ogre dashed in front of the warrior. Watanabe's eyes grew large with wonder – the ogre was taller than the great gate, his eyes were flashing like mirrors, and his huge mouth was wide open, flames of fire shooting out of it as he breathed.

Watanabe never flinched. He attacked the ogre with all his strength, and they fought face to face for a long time. At last the ogre, finding that he could neither frighten nor beat Watanabe and that he might himself be beaten, took flight. But Watanabe, determined not to let the monster escape, put spurs to his horse and gave chase. But though the knight rode fast, the ogre ran faster, and to his disappointment Watanabe found himself unable to overtake the monster, who was gradually lost to sight.

Watanabe returned to the gate where the fierce fight had taken place, and got down from his horse. As he did so he stumbled upon something lying on the ground. Stooping to pick it up he found that it was one of the ogre's huge arms, which he must have cut off in the fight. His joy was great at having secured such a prize, for this was the best of all proofs of his adventure with the ogre. So he took it up and carried it home as a trophy of his victory.

When Watanabe got back, he showed the arm to his comrades. They called him the hero of their band and gave him a great feast. His wonderful deed soon travelled to Kyoto, and people from far and near came to see the ogre's arm.

Watanabe now began to grow uneasy as to how he should keep the arm in safety, for he knew that the ogre to whom it belonged was still alive. He felt sure that one day or other, as soon as the ogre got over his scare, he would come to try to get his arm back again. Therefore Watanabe had a box made of the strongest wood and banded with iron. In this he placed the arm, and then he sealed down the heavy lid, refusing to open it for anyone. He kept the box in his own room and took charge of it himself, never allowing it out of his sight.

Now one night he heard someone knocking at the porch, asking for admittance. When the servant went to the door to see who it was, there was only an old woman, very respectable in appearance. On being asked who she was and what was her business, the old woman replied with a smile that she had been nurse to the master of the house when he was a baby. If the lord of the house was at home she begged to be allowed to see him.

The servant left the old woman at the door and went to tell his master that his old nurse had come to see him. Watanabe thought it strange that she should come at that time of night. But at the thought of his old nurse, who had been like a foster mother to him and whom he had not seen for a long time, a very tender feeling sprang up for her in his heart. He ordered the servant to show her in.

The old woman was ushered into the room, and after the customary bows and greetings were over, she said, "Master, the report of your brave fight with the ogre at the Gate of Rashomon is so widely known that even your poor old nurse has heard of it. I am very proud to think that my master was so brave as to dare to cut off an ogre's arm. Before I die it is the great wish of my life to see this arm."

"No," said Watanabe, "I am sorry, but I cannot grant your request. Ogres are very revengeful creatures, and if I open the box he may suddenly appear and carry off his arm."

The woman pleaded, but Watanabe refused.

Then the old woman said, "Do you suspect me of being a spy sent by the ogre?"

"No, of course I do not suspect you of being the ogre's spy, for you are my old nurse," Watanabe said.

"Then you cannot refuse to show me the arm any longer," entreated the old woman. "It is the great wish of my heart to see for once in my life the arm of an ogre!"

Watanabe could not hold out in his refusal any longer, so he gave in at last. He led the way to his own room, the old woman following.

When they were both in the room Watanabe

shut the door. Then he went towards a big box which stood in a corner of the room, took off the heavy lid and called the old woman to come near.

"What is it like? Let me have a good look at it," said the old nurse, with a joyful face.

She came nearer and nearer, as if she were afraid, till she stood right against the box. Suddenly she plunged her hand into the box and seized the arm,

crying with a loud, fearful voice that made the entire room shake, "Oh, joy! I have got my arm back again!" And from an old woman she was suddenly transformed into the towering figure of the frightful ogre!

Watanabe sprang back and was unable to move for a moment, so great was his astonishment. But recognising the ogre who had attacked him at the Gate of Rashomon, he determined with his usual courage to put an end to him this time. He seized his sword, drew it out of its sheath in a flash and tried to cut the ogre down.

So quick was Watanabe that the creature had a narrow escape. But the ogre sprang up to the ceiling and, bursting through the roof, disappeared in the mist and clouds.

In this way the ogre escaped with his arm. The knight gnashed his teeth with disappointment, but that was all he could do. He waited in patience for another opportunity to dispatch the ogre. But the latter was afraid of Watanabe's great strength and daring, and never troubled Kyoto again. So once more the people of the city were able to go out without fear even at night time, and the brave deeds of Watanabe have never been forgotten.

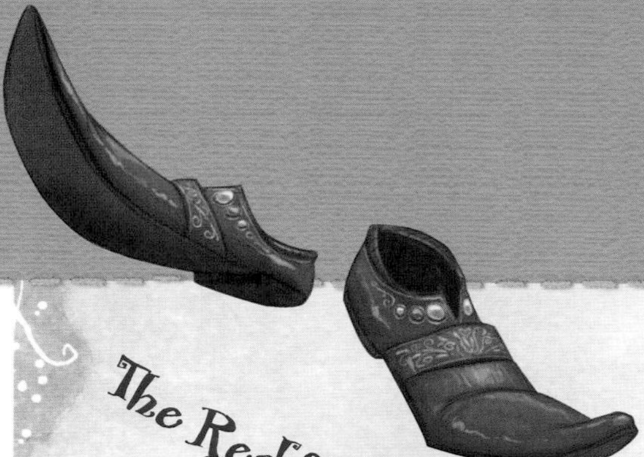

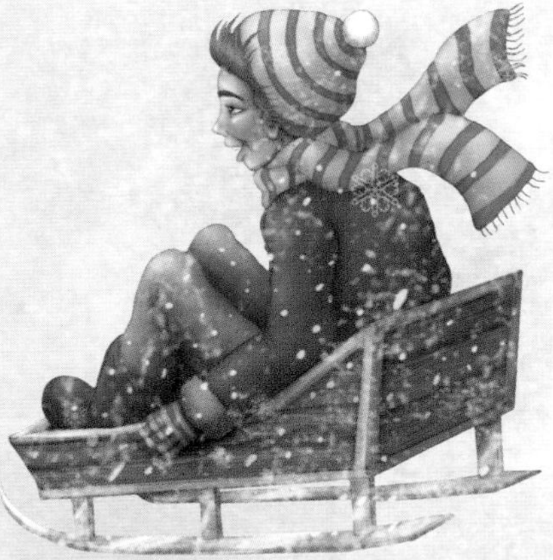

TRICKS AND MISHAPS

The Red Shoes

By Hans Christian Andersen

Once upon a time there was a little girl, pretty and dainty. But she was extremely poor – so poor that in summertime she was obliged to go barefooted because she had no sandals, and in winter she had to wear large wooden shoes, making her little toes go quite red.

In the middle of the village lived an old shoemaker's wife. She sat down and made, as well as she could, a pair of little shoes out of some old pieces of red cloth. They were clumsy, but she meant well, for they were intended for the little girl, whose name was Karen.

Karen received the shoes and wore them for the first time on the day of her mother's funeral. They were certainly not suitable for mourning, but she had no others, so she put her bare feet into them and walked behind the humble coffin.

Just then a large carriage came by, and in it sat an old lady. She looked at the little girl and, taking pity on her, said to the clergyman, "Look here, if you will give me the little girl, I will take care of her."

Karen believed that this was all on account of the red shoes, but the old lady thought them hideous, so they were burned. Karen was dressed very neatly and cleanly, she was taught to read and to sew, and people said that she was pretty. But the mirror told her, "You are more than pretty – you are beautiful."

One day the queen was travelling through that part of the country and had her little daughter, who was a princess, with her. All the people, Karen among them, streamed towards the castle, where the little princess, in fine white clothes, stood before the window and allowed herself to be stared at. She wore neither a train nor a golden crown, but beautiful, red Morocco shoes. They were indeed much finer than those that the shoemaker's wife had sewn for little Karen. There is really nothing in the world that can be compared to red shoes!

Karen was now old enough to have a special ceremony at church called confirmation. For this important occasion she received some new clothes, and she was also to have new shoes. The rich shoemaker in the town took the measure of her little foot in his own room, in which there stood great glass cases full of pretty shoes and white slippers. It all looked very lovely, but the old lady could not see very well, and therefore did not get much pleasure out of it. Among the shoes stood a pair of red ones, like those which the princess had worn. The shoemaker said that they had been made for a count's daughter, but that they had not fitted her.

"I suppose they are of patent leather?" asked the old lady. "They shine so."

"Yes, they do shine," said Karen. They fitted her, and were bought. But the old lady knew nothing of them being red, for she would never have allowed Karen to be confirmed in bright, bold red shoes, as she was now to be.

Everybody looked at her feet. And the whole of the way from the church door to the choir it seemed to Karen as if even the ancient figures on the monuments, in their stiff collars and long black robes, had their eyes fixed on her red shoes. It was only of these that she thought when the clergyman laid his hand upon her head and spoke of the holy baptism, of the promise to God, and told her that she was now to be a grown-up

Christian. The organ pealed forth solemnly, and the sweet children's voices mingled with that of their old leader, but Karen thought only of her red shoes.

In the afternoon the old lady heard from everybody that Karen had worn red shoes. She said that it was a shocking thing to do, that it was very improper, and that Karen was always to go to church in future in black shoes, even if they were old.

On the following Sunday there was Communion at Mass. Karen looked first at the black shoes, then at the red ones – she looked at the red ones for a while, and then put them on.

The sun was shining gloriously, so Karen and the old lady went along the footpath through the corn, where it was rather dusty.

At the church door stood an old crippled soldier leaning on a crutch. He had a wonderfully long beard, more red than white, and he bowed down to the ground and asked the old lady whether he might wipe her shoes. Then Karen put out her little foot too.

"Dear me, what pretty dancing shoes!" said the soldier. "Sit fast, when you dance," said he, addressing the shoes, and slapping the soles with his hand. The old lady gave the soldier some money and then went with Karen into the church.

And all the people inside looked at Karen's red shoes, and all the figures gazed at them. When Karen knelt before the altar and put the golden goblet to her mouth, she thought only of the red shoes. It seemed to her as though they were swimming about in the goblet, and she forgot to sing the hymns, and forgot to say the Lord's Prayer.

Now everyone came out of church, and the old lady stepped into her carriage. But just as Karen was lifting up her foot to get in too, the old soldier said, "Dear me, what pretty dancing shoes!" and Karen could not help it, she was obliged to dance a few steps. And when she had once begun, her legs continued to dance. It seemed as if the shoes had got power over them. She danced round the church corner, for she could not stop. The coachman had to

run after her and seize her. He lifted
her into the carriage, but her feet
continued to dance, so that
she kicked the good old
lady. At last they took

off her shoes and her legs were at rest.

At home the shoes were put into the cupboard, but Karen could not help looking at them.

Now the old lady fell ill, and it was said that she would not rise from her bed again. She had to be nursed and waited upon, and this was no one's duty more than Karen's. But there was a grand ball in the town, and Karen was invited. She looked at the red shoes, saying to herself that there was no sin in doing that. She put the red shoes on, thinking there was no harm in that either. And then she went to the ball, and commenced to dance.

But when she wanted to go to the right, the shoes danced to the left, and when she wanted to dance up the room, the shoes danced down the room, down the stairs, through the street, and out through the gates of the town. Karen danced, and was obliged to dance, far out into the dark wood. Suddenly something shone up among the trees, and she believed it was the moon, for it was a face. But it was the old soldier with the red beard. He sat there nodding his head and said, "Dear me, what pretty dancing shoes!"

Karen was frightened, and wanted to throw the red shoes away, but they stuck fast. She danced, and was obliged to go on dancing over field and meadow, in rain and sunshine, by night and by day – but by night it was most horrible.

She danced out into the open churchyard, but the dead there did not dance. They had something better to do than that. She wanted to sit down on the pauper's grave where the bitter fern grows, but for her there was neither peace nor rest. And as she danced past the open church door she saw an angel there in long white robes, with wings reaching from his shoulders down to the earth. His face was stern and grave, and in his hand he held a broad, shining sword.

"Dance you shall," said the angel to Karen, "dance in your red shoes till you are pale and cold. Dance you shall, from door to door, and where proud and wicked children live you shall knock, so that they may hear you and fear you! Dance you shall, dance!"

"Mercy!" cried Karen. But she did not hear what the angel answered, for the shoes carried her through the gate into the fields, along highways and byways, and unceasingly she had to dance.

One morning she danced past a door that she

knew well. They were singing a hymn inside, and a coffin was being carried out covered with flowers. Then she knew that she was forsaken by everyone and damned by the angel of God.

Karen danced, and was obliged to go on dancing through the dark night. The red shoes bore her away over thorns and stumps till she was all scratched and bruised. She danced away over the heath to a lonely little house. Here, she knew, lived the executioner. Karen tapped at the window and said, "Come out, come out! I cannot come in, for I must dance."

And the executioner answered, "I don't suppose you know who I am. I strike off the heads of the wicked, and I notice that my axe is tingling to do so now."

"Don't cut off my head," said Karen, "for then I could not repent of my sin. But cut off my feet with the red shoes!"

And then she confessed her sin, and the executioner struck off her feet with the red shoes.

But the shoes danced away with the little feet across the field into the deep forest.

Then he carved her a pair of wooden feet and some crutches, and taught her a hymn that is always sung by sinners. She kissed the hand that guided the axe and went away.

"Now, I have suffered enough for the red shoes," she said. "I will go to church, so that people can see me." And she went quickly up to the church door. But when she got there, the red shoes were dancing before her, and she was frightened, and turned back.

During the whole week she was sad and wept many bitter tears, but when Sunday came again she said, "Now I have suffered and striven enough. I believe I am quite as good as many of those who sit in church and give themselves airs." And so she went boldly on. But she had not got farther than the churchyard gate when she saw the red shoes dancing along before her. Then she became terrified and turned back, and repented right heartily of her sin.

Karen went to the parsonage, and begged that she might be taken into service there. She would be industrious, she said, and do everything that she could. She did not mind about the wages as long as she had a roof over her and was with good people. The pastor's wife had pity on her, and took her into service. And she was industrious and thoughtful. She sat quiet and listened when the pastor read aloud from the Bible in the evening. All the children liked her very much, but when they spoke about dress and grandeur and beauty she would shake her head.

On the following Sunday they all went to church, and she was asked whether she wished to go too. But, with tears in her eyes, she looked sadly at her crutches. And then the others went to hear God's Word, but she went alone into her little room, which was only large enough to hold the bed and a chair. Here she sat down with her hymn book, and as she was reading it with a pious mind, the wind carried the notes of the organ over to her from the church. In tears she lifted up her face and said, "O God, help me!"

Then the sun shone so brightly, and right before her stood an angel of God in white robes. It was the same one whom she had seen that night at the church door. He no longer carried the sharp sword, but a beautiful green branch, full of roses. With this he touched the ceiling, which rose up very high, and where he had touched it there shone a golden star. He touched the walls, which opened wide apart, and Karen saw the organ that was pealing forth. She saw the pictures of the old pastors and their wives, and the congregation sitting in the polished chairs and singing from their hymn books. The church itself had come to the poor girl in her narrow room, or the room had gone to the church. Karen sat in the pew with the rest of the pastor's household, and when they had finished the hymn and looked up, they nodded and said, "It was right of you to come, Karen."

"It was mercy," said she.

The organ played and the children's voices in the choir sounded soft and lovely. The bright, warm sunshine streamed through the window into the pew where Karen sat, and her heart became so filled with it, so filled with peace and joy, that it broke. Her soul flew on the sunbeams to heaven, and no one was there who asked after the red shoes.

The Snow Queen

An extract from the tale
by Hans Christian Andersen

Once upon a time there was a wicked sprite, who made a mirror that made all that was good and beautiful look poor and mean, while that which was good-for-nothing and ugly looked even more good-for-nothing and ugly. If a good thought passed through a man's mind, then a grin was seen in the mirror, and the sprite laughed heartily at his clever discovery. All the little sprites thought they would fly up to the sky and have a joke there. The higher they flew with the mirror, the more terribly it grinned – they could hardly hold it fast. Suddenly it shook so terribly with grinning, that it flew out of their hands and fell to the earth, where it was dashed in a hundred million and more pieces. And now it worked much more evil than before, for some of these pieces were hardly so large as a grain of sand. They flew into people's eyes and then people were attracted to what was evil. Some people even got a splinter in their heart, and then their heart became like a lump of ice. Many of the splinters were carried aloft by the air, and then blown about the wide world.

At this time, there lived in a large town two little children – a boy called Kay and a girl named Gerda. They were not brother and sister, but they cared for each other as much as if they were. Their houses were next to each other – and there was to the roof of each house a small window. In summer, when the windows were open they could get to each other with one jump over the gutter. The children liked nothing more than to sit together at the windows and talk, holding each other by the hand, often kissing the roses in their window boxes and looking up at the clear sunshine.

One day, Kay and Gerda were at the windows, looking at a picture book, when Kay said, "Oh! I feel such a sharp pain in my heart, and now something has got into my eye!"

Gerda put her arms around his neck. He winked his eyes and now there was nothing to be seen.

"I think it is out now," said he. But it was not. It was one of those pieces of glass from the magic mirror that had got into his eye, and poor Kay had got another piece right in his heart.

"You look so ugly!" he suddenly said to Gerda. "And these roses are very ugly, just like the boxes they are planted in!" And then he gave a box a good kick with his foot, and pulled a rose up.

"What are you doing?" cried the little girl. And as Kay perceived her fright, he pulled up another rose, got in at the window, and hastened off.

Afterwards, he was able to imitate the gait and manner of everyone in the street. Everything that was peculiar and displeasing in them, Kay knew how to imitate, and make everybody laugh – except the person being made fun of! But it was the glass he had got in his eye, the glass that was sticking in his heart, which made him tease even little Gerda, whose whole soul was devoted to him.

One winter's day, when flakes of snow were flying about, Kay spread the skirts of his coat, and caught the snow as it fell.

"Look through this glass, Gerda," said he. And every flake seemed larger, and appeared like a magnificent flower, or a beautiful star. It was splendid to look at!

"Look, how clever!" said Kay. "That's much more interesting than real flowers!"

It was not long after this, that Kay came one day with large gloves on, and his little sledge at his back, and bawled into Gerda's ears, "I have permission to go out into the square where the others are playing." And off he was in a moment.

There, in the market place, some of the boldest boys used to tie their sledges to the carts as they passed by, and so they were pulled

along, and got a good ride. Soon a large sledge
passed by. It was painted quite white, and there was
someone in it wrapped up in a rough white mantle
of fur, with a rough white fur cap on his head. The
sledge drove round the square twice, and Kay tied
on his sledge as quickly as he
could, and off he
drove with it.

On they went quicker and quicker into the next street. The person who drove turned round to Kay and nodded to him in a friendly manner, just as if they knew each other. Every time he was going to untie his sledge, the person nodded to him, and then Kay sat quiet.

And so on they went till they came outside the gates of the town. Then the snow began to fall so thickly that the little boy could not see an arm's length before him, but still on he went. Suddenly he let go of the string he held in his hand in order to get loose from the sledge, but it was no use – still the little vehicle rushed on with the quickness of the wind. Kay then cried as loud as he could, but no one heard him. The snow drifted and the sledge flew on, and sometimes it gave a jerk as though they were driving over hedges and ditches. Kay was quite frightened, and he tried to repeat the Lord's Prayer, but he was only able to remember his times tables.

The snowflakes grew larger and larger, till at last they looked just like great white fowls. Suddenly they flew on one side, the large sledge stopped, and the person who drove rose up. It was a lady. Her cloak and cap were of snow. She was tall and of slender figure, and of a dazzling whiteness. It was the Snow Queen.

"We have travelled fast," said she. "It is freezing cold. Come under my bearskin." And she put him in the sledge beside her, wrapped the fur round him, and he felt as though he were sinking in a snow drift.

"Are you still cold?" asked she, and then she kissed his forehead. Ah! It was colder than ice – it penetrated to his very heart, which was already almost a frozen lump. It seemed to Kay as if he were about to die – but a moment more and it was quite congenial to him, and he did not notice the cold that was around him.

"My sledge! Do not forget my sledge!" It was the first thing he thought of. It was there tied to one of the white chickens, who flew along with it on his back behind the large sledge. The Snow

Queen kissed Kay once more, and then he forgot little Gerda, grandmother, and all whom he had left at his home.

Kay thought she was very beautiful. In his eyes she was perfect, and he did not fear her at all. He looked upwards in the large, huge empty space above him, and on she flew with him, high over the black clouds, while the storm moaned and whistled as though it were singing some old tune. On they flew over woods and lakes, over seas, and many lands, and beneath them the chilling storm rushed fast, the wolves howled, the snow crackled. Above them flew large screaming crows, but higher up appeared the moon, quite large and bright. And it was on it that Kay gazed during the long, long winter's night, while by day he slept at the feet of the Snow Queen.

What became of little Gerda when Kay did not return? Where could he be? Nobody knew. Nobody could give any information. All the boys knew was that they had seen him tie his sledge to another

large, splendid one, which drove down the street and out of the town. Nobody knew where he was, many sad tears were shed, and little Gerda wept long and bitterly.

At last she said that he must have been drowned in the river that flowed close to the town – that alas, he must be dead.

The King who would see Paradise

From Andrew Lang's *Orange Fairy Book*

Once upon a time there was a king who came upon a holy man, or fakeer, in a lonely place in the mountains. The fakeer was seated on a little old bedstead reading the Koran, with his patched cloak thrown over his shoulders.

The king asked him what he was reading and the fakeer he was reading about Paradise, and praying that he might be worthy to enter there. Then they began to talk, and the king asked the fakeer if he could show him a glimpse of Paradise, for he found it impossible to believe in what he could not see. The fakeer replied that he was asking a very difficult and perhaps dangerous thing, but that he would pray for him, and perhaps he might be able to do it. But he warned the king against both the dangers of his unbelief and the curiosity that prompted him to ask this thing. However, the king was not to be swayed, and he promised the fakeer always to provide him with food, if he, in return, would pray for him. To this the fakeer agreed, and so they parted.

Time went on, and the king always sent the old fakeer his food according to his promise. But whenever he sent to ask him when he was going to show him Paradise, the fakeer always replied, "Not yet, not yet!"

After a year or two had passed, the king heard one day that the fakeer was very ill and believed to be dying. Instantly he hurried off and found that it was true, and that the fakeer was even then breathing his last. There and then the king besought him to remember his promise, and to show him a glimpse of Paradise. The dying fakeer replied that if the king would come to his funeral and, when the grave was filled in and everyone else had gone away, he would come and lay his hand upon the grave, he would keep his word and show him a glimpse of Paradise. At the same time he implored the king not to do this, but to be content to see Paradise when God called him there. Still the king's curiosity was so aroused that he would not give way.

After the fakeer was dead and had been buried, the king stayed behind when all the rest went away. Then, when he was quite alone, he stepped forward and laid his hand upon the grave. Instantly the ground opened and the astonished king peered in. He saw a flight of rough steps and, at the bottom of them, the fakeer sitting, just as he used to sit, on his rickety bedstead, reading the Koran!

At first the king was so surprised and frightened that he could only stare. But the fakeer beckoned to him to come down, so, mustering up his courage, he boldly stepped down into the grave.

The fakeer rose and, making a sign to the king to follow, walked a few paces along a dark passage. Then he stopped, turned solemnly to his companion and, with a movement of his hand, drew aside a heavy curtain, revealing – what? No one knows what was there, shown to the king. But when the fakeer at length dropped the curtain and

the king turned to leave the place, he had had his glimpse of Paradise! Trembling in every limb, he staggered back along the passage and stumbled up the steps, out of the tomb into the fresh air again.

The dawn was breaking. It seemed odd to the king that he had been so long in the grave. It appeared only a few minutes ago that he had descended, passed along a few steps to the place where he had peeped beyond the curtain, and returned again after perhaps five minutes of that wonderful view. And what was it he had seen? He racked his brains to remember, but he could not call to mind a single thing.

How curious everything looked too! His own city, which he was now entering, seemed changed and strange to him. The sun was already up when he turned into the palace gate and entered the hall. A chamberlain came across and asked him why he sat unbidden in the king's presence.

"But I am the king!" he cried.

"What king?" said the chamberlain.

"The true king of this country," he replied.
Then the chamberlain went away and spoke to
the king who sat on the throne, and the old king
heard words like "mad", "age" and "compassion".
The king on the throne called him to come
forward and, as he went, he caught sight of
himself reflected in the polished steel shield
of the bodyguard, and he started back in
horror! He was old, dirty, and ragged!
His long white beard and locks were
unkempt, and straggled all over his
chest and shoulders. Only one sign
of royalty remained to him, and
that was the signet ring upon his
right hand. He dragged it off
with shaking fingers and held it
up to the king.

"Tell me who I am," the old
king cried. "There is my
signet, which once sat where
you sit – even yesterday!"

The king looked at him compassionately and examined the signet ring with curiosity. Then he looked at dusty records and archives of the kingdom, and old coins of previous reigns, and compared them faithfully.

At last the king turned to the old man and said, "Such a king as this, whose signet ring you have, reigned seven hundred years ago. But he is said to have disappeared. Where did you get the ring?"

Then the old man understood that he, who was not content to wait patiently to see Paradise, had been judged already. He turned and left the hall without a word, and went into the jungle.

Here he lived a life of prayer and meditation for twenty-five years, until at last the Angel of Death came to him, and mercifully released him, purged and purified through his punishment.

The Devil
and his
Grandmother

By the Brothers Grimm

Here was a great war, and the king had many soldiers. But he gave them small pay, so small that they could not live upon it, so three of them agreed among themselves to desert.

One of them said to the others, "If we are caught we shall be hanged on the gallows. How shall we manage it?"

Another said, "Look at that great cornfield. If we were to hide ourselves there, no one could find us. The troops are not allowed to enter it, and tomorrow they are to march away."

So the soldiers crept into the corn, only the troops did not march away, but remained lying all round about it. They stayed in the corn for two days and two nights, and were so hungry that they all but died, but if they had come out, their death would have been certain.

Then the three soldiers said, "What is the use of our deserting if we have to perish so miserably in this cornfield?"

But now a fiery dragon came flying through the air, and it came down to them, and asked why they had hidden themselves there.

They answered, "We are three soldiers who have deserted because the pay was so bad. But now we shall have to die of hunger if we stay here, or dangle on the gallows if we go out."

"If you will serve me for seven years," said the dragon, "I will carry you through the army so that no one shall seize you."

"We have no choice, so we have to accept," the soldiers replied.

Then the dragon caught hold of them
with his claws, and carried them away
through the air over the army, and
put them down again on the
earth far from it. But the
dragon was no other than
the Devil. He gave them a
small whip and said,
"Whip with it and crack
it, and then as much
gold will spring up
round about as you can
wish for. Then you can live
like great lords, keep horses, and drive your
carriages, but when the seven years have come to an
end, you are my property." Then he put in front of
them a book that they were all three forced to sign.
"I will, however, then set you a riddle," said the
dragon, "and if you can guess that, you shall be free,
and released from my power."

Then the dragon flew away from them, and they

went away with their whip, had gold in plenty, ordered themselves rich clothes, and travelled about the world. Wherever they were they lived in pleasure and magnificence, rode on horseback, drove in carriages, ate and drank, but did nothing at all wicked.

The time slipped quickly away, and when the seven years were coming to an end, two of them were terribly anxious and alarmed, but the third took matters easily, and said, "Brothers, fear nothing. My head is sharp enough – I shall guess the riddle." They went out into the open country and sat down, and the two pulled sorrowful faces.

Then an old woman came up to them who enquired why they were so sad.

"Alas!" said they. "How can that concern you? After all, you cannot help us."

"Who knows?" she replied. "Confide your trouble to me."

So they told the old woman that they had been the Devil's servants for nearly seven years, and that he had provided them with gold as plentifully as if it had been blackberries. But that they had sold themselves to the Devil, and were forfeited to him, if at the end of the seven years they could not guess a riddle.

The old woman said, "If you are to be saved, one of you must go into the forest. There he will come to a fallen rock that looks like a little house. He must enter that, and then he will obtain help."

The two melancholy ones thought to themselves, 'That will still not save us,' and stayed where they were. But the third one, the merry one, got up and walked on into the forest until he arrived at the rock-house.

In the little house, however, a very old woman was sitting, who was the Devil's grandmother. She asked the soldier where he came from, and what he wanted there. He told her everything that had happened and, as he pleased her well, she had pity on him, and said she would help him.

The grandmother lifted up a great stone that lay above a cellar, and said, "Hide yourself there. You can hear everything that is said here. Only sit still, and do not stir. When the dragon comes, I will question him about the riddle. He tells everything to me, so listen carefully to his answer."

At twelve o' clock at night, the dragon came flying there and asked for his dinner. The grandmother laid the table and served up food and drink, so that he was pleased, and they ate and drank together. In the course of conversation, she asked him what kind of a day he had had, and how many souls he had got.

"Nothing went very well today," the dragon answered, "but I have laid hold of three soldiers. I have them safe."

"Indeed! Three soldiers. That's something, but they may escape you yet."

The Devil said mockingly, "They are mine! I will set them a riddle, which they will never in this world be able to guess!"

"What riddle is that?" she enquired.

"I will tell you. In the great North Sea lies a dead dogfish, that shall be your roast meat, and the rib of a whale shall be your silver spoon, and a hollow old horse's hoof shall be your wine glass."

When the Devil had gone to bed, the old grandmother raised up the stone and let out the soldier. "Did you pay careful attention to everything?" she asked.

"Yes," said he, "I know enough."

Then he had to go back another way, through the window, secretly and with all speed to his companions. He told them how the Devil had been tricked by the old grandmother, and how he had learned the answer to the riddle from him. Then they were all joyous and of good cheer, and took the whip and whipped so much gold for themselves that it ran all over the ground.

When the seven years had fully gone by, the Devil came with the book, showed the signatures, and said, "I will take you with me to hell. There you shall have a meal. If you can guess what kind of roast meat you will have to eat, you shall be free and released from your bargain, and may keep the whip as well."

Then the first soldier began and said, "In the great North Sea lies a dead dogfish, that no doubt is the roast meat."

The Devil was angry, and began to mutter, "Hm! Hm! Hm!" And he asked the second, "But what will your spoon be?"

"The rib of a whale, that is to be our silver spoon," the second soldier answered.

The Devil made a wry face, again growled, "Hm!

Hm! Hm!" and said to the third, "And do you also know what your wine glass is to be?"

"An old horse's hoof is to be our wine glass."

Then the Devil flew away with a loud cry, and had no more power over them. But the three kept the whip, whipped as much money for themselves as they wanted, and lived happily to their end.

The Ratcatcher

From Andrew Lang's *Red Fairy Book*

A very long time ago the town of Hamel in Germany was invaded by bands of rats, the like of which had never been seen before nor will ever be seen again.

They were great black creatures that ran boldly in broad daylight through the streets, and swarmed all over the houses, so that people could not put their hand or foot down anywhere without touching one. When dressing in the morning they found them in their breeches and petticoats, in their pockets and in their boots. And when they wanted a morsel to eat, the voracious horde had swept away everything from cellar to garret. The night was even worse. As soon as the lights were out, these untiring nibblers set to work. And everywhere, in the ceilings, in the floors, in the cupboards, there was a chase and a rummage, and so furious a noise, that a deaf man could not have rested for one hour together.

Neither cats nor dogs, nor poison nor traps, nor prayers nor candles burned to all the saints – nothing would do anything. The more they killed the more came. And the inhabitants of Hamel began to go to the dogs (not that they were of much use), when one Friday there arrived in the town a man with a queer face, who played the bagpipes and sang this refrain:

"Qui vivra verra:
Le voila,
Le preneur des rats."

He was a great gawky fellow, with a crooked nose, a long rat-tail moustache, and two great yellow piercing and mocking eyes, under a large felt hat set off by a scarlet cock's feather. He was dressed in a green jacket with a leather belt and red breeches, and on his feet were sandals fastened by thongs passed round his legs in the gipsy fashion. That is how he may be seen to this day, painted on a window of the cathedral of Hamel.

He stopped on the great market-place before the

town hall, turned his back on the church and went on with his music, singing:

"Who lives shall see:

This is he,

The ratcatcher."

The town council had just assembled to consider once more this plague, from which no one could save the town.

The stranger sent word to the counsellors that, if they would make it worth his while, he would rid them of all their rats before night, down to the very last one.

"Then he is a sorcerer!" cried the citizens with one voice. "We must beware of him."

The Town Counsellor, who was considered clever, reassured them.

He said, "Sorcerer or not, if this bagpiper speaks the truth, it was he who sent us this horrible vermin that he wants to rid us of today for money. Well, we must learn to catch the Devil in his own snares. You leave it to me."

"Leave it to the Town Counsellor," said the citizens one to another.

And the stranger was brought before them.

"Before night," said the stranger, "I shall have despatched all the rats in Hamel if you will but pay me a gros a head."

"A gros a head!" cried the citizens. "But that will come to millions of florins!"

The Town Counsellor simply shrugged his shoulders and said to the stranger, "A bargain! To work! The rats will be paid one gros a head."

The bagpiper announced that he would operate that very evening when the moon rose. He added that the inhabitants should at that hour leave the streets free, and content themselves with looking out of their windows at what was passing, and that it would be a pleasant spectacle.

When the people of Hamel heard of the bargain, they too exclaimed, "A gros a head! But this will cost us a deal of money!"

"Leave it to the Town Counsellor," said the town

council with a malicious air. And the good people of Hamel repeated with their counsellors, "Leave it to the Town Counsellor."

Towards nine at night the bagpiper reappeared on the market-place. He turned his back on the church, and the moment the moon rose on the horizon, "Trarira, trari!" the bagpipes resounded.

It was first a slow, caressing sound, then more and more lively and urgent, and so sonorous and piercing that it penetrated as far as the farthest alleys and retreats of the town.

Soon from the bottom of the cellars, the top of the garrets, from under all the furniture, from all the nooks and corners of the houses, out came the rats, searching for the doors, flinging themselves into the street, and beginning to run in file towards the front of the town hall, so squeezed together that they covered the pavement like waves.

When the square was quite full the bagpiper faced about and, still playing briskly, turned towards the river that runs at the foot of the walls of Hamel.

When he arrived there he turned round – the rats were following.

"Hop! Hop!" he cried, pointing with his finger to the middle of the stream, where the water whirled and was drawn down as if through a funnel. And hop! Hop! Without hesitating, the rats took the leap, swam straight to the funnel, plunged in head foremost and disappeared.

The plunging continued till midnight.

At last, dragging himself with difficulty, there came a big rat, white with age, and it stopped on the bank. It was the king of the band.

"Are they all there, friend Blanchet?" the bagpiper asked the big rat.

"They are all there," replied friend Blanchet.

"And how many were they?"

"Nine hundred and ninety thousand, nine hundred and ninety-nine."

"Then go and join them, old sire, and au revoir."

Then the old white rat sprang in his turn into the river, swam to the whirlpool and disappeared.

When the bagpiper had thus concluded his business he went to bed at his inn. And for the first time during three months, the people of Hamel slept quietly through the night.

The next morning, at nine o' clock, the bagpiper went to the town hall, where the town council were waiting for him.

"All your rats took a jump into the river last night," said he to the counsellors, "and I guarantee that not one of them comes back. They were nine hundred and ninety thousand, nine hundred and ninety-nine, at one gros a head. Reckon!"

"Let us reckon the heads first. One gros a head is one head the gros. Where are the heads?"

The ratcatcher did not expect this treacherous stroke. He paled with anger and his eyes flashed fire. "The heads!" cried he. "If you care about them, go and find them in the river."

"So," replied the Town Counsellor, "you refuse to hold to the terms of your agreement? We ourselves could refuse you all payment. But you have been of use to us, and we will not let you go without a recompense," and he offered him fifty crowns.

"Keep your recompense for yourself," replied the ratcatcher proudly. "If you do not pay me I will be paid by your heirs."

Thereupon he pulled his hat down over his eyes, went hastily out of the hall, and left the town without speaking to a soul.

When the Hamel people heard how the affair had ended they rubbed their hands, and with no more scruple than their Town Counsellor, they laughed over the ratcatcher, who, they said, was caught in his own trap. But what made them laugh above all was his threat of getting himself paid by their heirs. Ha! They wished that they only had such creditors for the rest of their lives.

Next day, which was a Sunday, they all went gaily to church, thinking that after Mass they would at last be able to eat some good thing that the rats had not tasted before them. They never suspected the terrible surprise that awaited them on their return home. No children anywhere – they had all disappeared!

"Our children! Where are our poor children?" was the cry that was soon heard in all the streets.

Then through the east door of the town came three children, who cried and wept, and this is what they told. While the parents were at church a wonderful music had resounded. Soon all the little boys and all the little girls that had been left at home had gone out, attracted by the magic sounds, and had rushed to the great market-place. There they found the ratcatcher playing his bagpipes at the same spot as the evening before. Then the stranger had begun to walk quickly, and they had followed, running, singing and dancing to the sound of the music, as far as the foot of the mountain that one sees on entering Hamel. At their approach the mountain had opened a little, and the bagpiper and children had gone in, after which it had closed again. Only the three little ones who told the adventure had remained outside, as if by a miracle. One was bandy-legged and could not run fast enough. The other, who had left the house in haste, one foot shod the other bare, had hurt himself against a big stone and could not walk without difficulty. The third had arrived in time, but in hurrying to go in with the others, had struck so violently against the wall of the

mountain that he fell backwards at the very moment it closed.

At this story the parents redoubled their lamentations. They all ran with pikes and mattocks to the foot of the mountain, and searched till evening to find the opening by which their children had disappeared. But they were not able to find it. At last, with the night falling, they returned desolate to Hamel.

But the most unhappy of all was the Town Counsellor, for he lost three little boys and two pretty little girls, and to crown all, the people of Hamel overwhelmed him with reproaches, forgetting that the evening before they had all agreed with him.

But what had become of all these poor children of Hamel?

The parents always hoped they were not dead, and that the ratcatcher, who certainly must have come out of the mountain, would have taken them with him to his country. That is why for several years they went in search of them to different countries, but no one ever came on the trace of the poor little ones.

The Singing Bone

By the Brothers Grimm

*I*n a certain country there was once great lamentation over a wild boar that laid waste the farmers' fields, killed the cattle and attacked people with its tusks.

The king promised a large reward to anyone who would free the land from this plague, but the beast was so big and strong that no one dared to go near the forest in which it lived. At last the king gave notice that whosoever should capture or kill the wild boar should have his only daughter for his wife.

Now there lived in the country two brothers, sons of a poor man, who declared themselves willing to undertake the hazardous enterprise – the elder, who was crafty and shrewd, out of pride, and the younger, who was innocent and simple, from a kind heart.

The king said to the two brothers, "In order that you may be the more sure of finding the beast, you must go into the forest in which it lives from opposite sides."

So the elder went in on the west side, and the younger on the east.

When the younger brother had gone a short way, a little man stepped up to him. He held in his hand a spear and said, "I give you this spear because your heart is pure and good. With this spear you can boldly attack the wild boar, and it will do you no harm."

The younger brother thanked the little man, shouldered the spear, and went on fearlessly through the forest.

Before long he saw the beast, which rushed at
him, but he held the spear towards it, and in its
blind fury it ran so swiftly against it that its
heart was split in two. Then he took the
monster on his back and went
homewards with it to the king.

As he came out at the other side of the wood,
there stood at the entrance a house where people
were making merry with wine and dancing. His
elder brother had gone in here, and, thinking that
after all the boar would not run away from him, was
going to drink until he felt brave. But when he saw
his young brother coming out of the wood laden

with his booty, his envious, evil heart gave him no peace. He called out to him, "Come in, dear brother, rest and refresh yourself with a cup of wine."

The youth, who suspected no evil, went in and told him about the good little man who had given him the spear wherewith he had slain the boar.

The elder brother kept him there until the evening, and then they went away together. When in the darkness they came to a bridge over a brook, the elder brother let the other go first. When the younger brother was halfway across, the elder brother gave him such a blow from behind that the younger fell down dead. The elder buried him beneath the bridge, took the boar, and carried it to the king, pretending that he had killed it, whereupon he obtained the king's daughter in marriage. And when his younger brother did not come back he said, "The boar must have killed him," and everyone believed it.

But as nothing remains hidden from God, so this black deed also was to come to light.

Years afterwards a shepherd was driving his herd across the bridge, and saw lying in the sand beneath, a snow-white little bone. He thought that it would make a good mouthpiece, so he clambered down, picked it up, and cut out of it a mouthpiece for his horn. But when he blew through it the first time, to his great astonishment, the bone began of its own accord to sing:

"Ah, friend, thou blowest upon my bone!
Long have I lain beside the water.
My brother slew me for the boar,
And took for his wife the king's daughter."

"What a wonderful horn!" said the shepherd.

"It sings by itself. I must take it to my lord the king."

And when he came with it to the king the horn again began to sing its song. The king understood it all, and caused the ground below the bridge to be dug up, and then the whole skeleton of the murdered man came to light. The wicked brother could not deny the deed, and was imprisoned for life. But the bones of the brother were laid to rest in a beautiful tomb in the churchyard.

BÄD BEÄSTIES

Little Red Riding Hood

By the Brothers Grimm

Once upon a time there was a dear little girl who was loved by everyone who looked at her, but most of all by her grandmother, and there was nothing that she would not have given to the child. Once she gave her a little riding hood of red velvet, which suited the little girl so well that she would never wear anything else. So from that day forward she was always called 'Little Red Riding Hood'.

One day her mother said to her, "Come, Little Red Riding Hood, here is a piece of cake and a bottle of wine – take them to your grandmother.

She is ill and weak, and they will do her good. Set out before it gets hot, and when you are going, walk nicely and quietly and do not run off the path, or you may fall and break the bottle. And when you go into her room, don't forget to say, 'Good morning,' and don't peep into every corner before you do it."

"I will take great care," said Little Red Riding Hood to her mother.

The grandmother lived out in the wood, half a league from the village, and just as Little Red Riding Hood entered the wood, a wolf met her. She did not know what a wicked creature he was, and was not at all afraid of him.

"Good day, Little Red Riding Hood," said he.

"Thank you kindly, wolf."

"Where are you going so early, Little Red Riding Hood?"

"To my grandmother's."

"What have you got in your apron?"

"Cake and wine. Yesterday was baking day, so poor sick grandmother is to have something good, to make her stronger."

"Where does your grandmother live, Little Red Riding Hood?"

"A good quarter of a league farther on in the wood. Her house stands under the three large oak trees, and the nut trees are just below. You surely must know it," replied Little Red Riding Hood.

The wolf thought to himself, 'What a tender young creature! What a nice plump mouthful! She will be better to eat than the old woman. I must act craftily, so as to catch both.'

So the wolf walked for a short time by the side of Little Red Riding Hood, and then he said to her, "See how pretty the flowers are about here – why do you not look round Little Red Riding Hood? I believe, too, that you do not hear how sweetly the little birds are singing. You walk gravely along as if you were going to school, while everything else out here in the wood is merry."

Little Red Riding Hood raised her eyes, and when she saw the sunbeams dancing here and there

through the trees, and pretty flowers growing everywhere, she thought, 'Suppose I take grandmother a fresh nosegay – that would please her too. It is so early in the day that I shall still get there in good time.'

So she ran from the path into the wood to look for flowers. And whenever she had picked one, she fancied that she saw a still prettier one farther on, and ran after it. So Little Red Riding Hood got deeper and deeper into the wood.

Meanwhile the wolf ran straight to the grandmother's house and knocked at the door.

"Who is there?"

"Little Red Riding Hood," replied the wolf. "She is bringing cake and wine. Open the door."

"Lift the latch," called out the grandmother, "I am too weak, and cannot get up."

The wolf lifted the latch, the door sprang open, and without saying a word, he went straight to the grandmother's bed and devoured her. Then he put on her cap and laid himself in the bed.

Little Red Riding Hood, however, had been running about picking flowers, and when she had gathered so many that she could carry no more, she remembered her grandmother, and set out on the way to her.

Little Red Riding Hood was surprised to find the cottage door standing open, and when she went into the room, she had such a strange feeling that she said to herself, "Oh dear! How uneasy I feel today, and at other times I like being with grandmother so much."

Little Red Riding Hood called out, "Good morning," but received no answer. So she went to the bed. There lay her grandmother with her cap pulled far over her face, and looking very strange.

"Oh, Grandmother," Little Red Riding Hood said, "what big ears you have!"

"All the better to hear you with," was the reply.

"But, Grandmother, what big eyes you have!"

"All the better to see you with."

"But, Grandmother, what large hands you have!"

"All the better to hug you with."

"Oh but, Grandmother, what a terrible big mouth you have!"

"All the better to eat you with!"

And scarcely had the wolf said this, than with one bound he was out of the bed and had swallowed up Little Red Riding Hood.

When the wolf had appeased his appetite, he lay down again in the bed, fell asleep and began to snore very loudly.

A huntsman was just passing the house, and thought to himself, 'How the old woman is snoring! I must just see if she wants anything.' So he went into the room, and when he came to the bed, he saw that the wolf was lying in it.

"Do I find you here, you monster!" said he. "I have long sought you!" But just as the huntsman was going to fire at the wolf, it occurred to him that the wolf might have devoured the grandmother, and that she might still be saved. So he did not fire, but took a pair of scissors, and began to cut open the stomach of the sleeping wolf.

When the huntsman had made two snips, he saw the little red riding hood shining, and then he made two more snips, and the little girl sprang out, crying, "Ah, how frightened I have been! How dark it was inside the wolf."

After that the grandmother came out alive also, but scarcely able to breathe. Little Red Riding Hood, however, quickly fetched great stones with which they filled the wolf's belly, and when he

awoke, he wanted to run away, but the stones were so heavy that he collapsed at once, and fell dead.

Then all three were delighted. The huntsman drew off the wolf's skin and went home with it. The grandmother ate the cake and drank the wine that Little Red Riding Hood had brought, and felt much better. And Little Red Riding Hood thought to herself, 'As long as I live, I will never leave the path by myself to run into the wood, when my mother has forbidden me to do so.'

It is also related that once, when Little Red Riding Hood was again taking cakes to her grandmother, another wolf spoke to her, and tried to entice her from the path. Little Red Riding Hood, however, was on her guard, and carried on her way. She told her grandmother that she had met the wolf, and that he had said good morning to her, but with such a wicked look in his eyes, that if they had not been on the public path she was certain he would have eaten her up.

"Well," said the grandmother, "we will shut the door, so that he cannot come in."

Soon afterwards the wolf knocked, and cried, "Open the door, Grandmother, I am Little Red Riding Hood, and am bringing you some cakes."

But they did not speak or open the door. So the wolf stole twice or thrice round the house, and at last jumped on the roof. He intended to wait until Little Red Riding Hood went home in the evening, and then to steal after her and devour her in the darkness. But the grandmother knew what was in his thoughts.

In front of the house was a great stone trough, so she said to Little Red Riding Hood, "Take the pail. I made some sausages yesterday, so carry the water in which I boiled them to the trough."

Little Red Riding Hood carried the water until the great trough was quite full. Then the smell of the sausages reached the wolf. He sniffed and peeped down, and at last stretched out his neck so far that he could no longer keep his footing and began to slip. He slipped down from the roof straight into the great trough, and was drowned. So Little Red Riding Hood went happily home, and no one ever did anything to harm her again.

Schippeitaro

From *Tales of Wonder Every Child Should Know*
by Kate Douglas Wiggin and Nora Archibald Smith

*L*ong, long ago, in the days of fairies and giants, ogres and dragons, valiant knights and distressed damsels, a brave young warrior went out into the wide world in search of adventures.

He travelled over hill and down dale, and for some time he went on without meeting with anything out of the ordinary. But at length, after journeying through a thick forest, he found himself one evening on a wild and lonely mountainside. No village was in sight, no cottage, not even the hut of a charcoal burner, so often to be found on the outskirts of the forest. He had been following a faint and much overgrown path, but at length, even that was lost sight of in the dense undergrowth.

Twilight was coming on, and in vain he strove to recover the lost track. Each effort seemed only to entangle him more hopelessly in the briers, ferns and tall grasses that grew thickly on all sides.

Faint and weary he stumbled on in the fast gathering darkness, until suddenly he came upon an eerie little temple, deserted and half ruined, but which still contained a shrine. Here at least was shelter from the chilly dews and, though the sinister appearance of the temple made the hairs stand up on the back of his neck, he decided to spend the night here. He had no food, but wrapped in his thick mantle, and with his good sword by his side, he lay down and was soon fast asleep.

Toward midnight he was awakened by a dreadful noise. At first he thought it must be a dream, but the noise continued, the whole place resounding with the most terrible shrieks and yells. The warrior

raised himself cautiously and, seizing his sword, peeped quietly through a hole in the ruined wall.

He beheld a strange and awful sight. A troop of hideous cats were engaged in a wild and horrible dance, their yells and howling echoing through the night. Mingled with their unearthly cries the young warrior could clearly distinguish the words:

"Tell it not to Schippeitaro! Listen for his bark!

Tell it not to Schippeitaro! Keep it close and dark!"

A beautiful, clear full moon shed its light upon this gruesome scene, which the bold young warrior watched with amazement and horror. Suddenly, the midnight hour passed, and the phantom cats disappeared and all was silent once more.

The rest of the night passed undisturbed, and the young warrior slept soundly until morning. When he awoke the sun was already up, and he hastened to leave the strange scene of last night's adventure. By the bright morning light he presently discovered traces of a path, which the evening before had been invisible. This he followed and found to his great joy that it led, not as he had feared, to the forest through which he had come the day before, but in the opposite direction toward an open plain. There he saw one or two scattered cottages and, a little farther on, a village.

Pressed by an awful hunger that was gnawing away at his stomach, he was making his way toward the village when he heard the tones of a woman's voice, loud in wailing and pleading. No sooner did these sounds of distress reach the warrior's ears than his hunger was forgotten, and he hurried on to the nearest cottage to find out what was the matter and if he could give any help.

The people listened to his questions, and shaking their heads sorrowfully, told him that all help was in vain. "Every year," said they, "the mountain spirit claims a victim. The time has come, and this very night he will devour our loveliest maiden. This is the cause of all our weeping."

And when the young warrior enquired further, they told him that at sunset the victim would be put into a wooden chest, carried to that very ruined temple where he had passed the night, and there left alone. In the morning she would have vanished. So it was each year, and so it would be now – there was no help for it.

The young warrior had a noble heart, and as he listened he was filled with an earnest desire to rescue the maiden. And, the mention of the ruined temple having brought back to his mind the adventure of the night before, he asked the people whether they had ever heard the name of Schippeitaro, and who and what he was.

"Schippeitaro is a strong and beautiful dog," was the reply. "He belongs to the head man of our prince who lives only a little way from here. We often see him following his master. He is a fine and brave fellow."

The young knight did not stop to ask more questions, but hurried off to Schippeitaro's master and begged him to lend him his dog for one night. The dog's master listened carefully to the warrior's strange tale, but at first was unwilling to agree to his request. At length, however, he agreed to lend Schippeitaro on condition that he should be brought back the next day. Overjoyed, the young warrior led the dog away.

Next he went to see the parents of the unhappy maiden who was to be left out for the sacrifice. The warrior told them to keep their daughter safely in the house and watch her carefully until his return. He then placed the dog Schippeitaro in the chest that had been prepared for the maiden, and, with the help of some of the young men of the village, carried it to the ruined temple, and there set it down. The young men refused to stay one moment on that haunted spot, but hurried down the mountain as if the whole troop of hobgoblins had been at their heels. However, the young warrior, with no companion but the dog, stayed to see what would happen.

The valiant knight waited alone in the dark and the cold, peering into the shadows, alert for any snap of twig or rustle of undergrowth to alert him to an approach. He waited, watched and listened, listened, watched and waited, until at midnight, when the full moon was high in the sky and shed its light over the mountain, the phantom cats came once more. This time they had in their midst a huge, black tomcat, fiercer and more terrible than all the rest, which the young warrior had no difficulty in knowing as the frightful mountain fiend himself. No sooner did this monster catch sight of the chest

than he danced and sprang round it, with yells of
triumph and joy, followed by his companions.
When he had long enough jeered at and taunted his
victim, he threw open the chest.

But this time the tomcat met his match. The brave Schippeitaro sprang upon him, and seizing him with his teeth, held him fast, while the young warrior with one stroke of his good sword laid the monster dead at his feet.

As for the other cats, too much astonished to flee, they stood gazing at their dead leader, and were made short work of by the knight and Schippeitaro.

The young warrior brought back the brave dog to his master with a thousand thanks. He then told the father and mother of the maiden that their daughter was free, and the people of the village that the fiend had claimed his last victim, and would trouble them no more.

"You owe all this to the brave Schippeitaro," he said as he bade them farewell, and went his way in search of fresh adventures.

The Farmer and the Badger

From *Japanese Fairy Tales*
by Yei Theodora Ozaki

Long, long ago in the distant country of Japan, there lived an old farmer and his wife who had made their home in the mountains, far from any town. Their only neighbour was a bad and malicious badger. This badger used to come out every night, whether moonlit or dark, and run across to the farmer's field. He would spoil the vegetables and the rice that the farmer spent his time carefully cultivating.

The badger at last grew so ruthless in his mischievous work, and did so much harm everywhere on the farm, that the good-natured farmer could not stand it any longer, and determined to put a stop to it. So he lay in wait day after day and night after night, hoping to catch the badger, but all in vain. Then he laid traps for the wicked animal.

The farmer's trouble and patience was rewarded, for one fine day on going about his rounds, he found the badger caught in a hole he had dug and disguised for that purpose. The farmer was delighted at having caught his enemy, and carried him home securely bound with rope.

When he reached the house the farmer said to his wife, "I have at last caught the bad badger. You must keep an eye on him while I am out at work and not let him escape, because I want to get my revenge on him and have hot badger soup for supper tonight." Saying this, he hung the badger up to the rafters of his storehouse and went out to his work in the fields.

The badger was in great distress, for he did not at

all like the idea of being made into soup that night, and he thought for a long time, trying to hit upon some plan by which he might escape. It was hard to think clearly in his uncomfortable position, for he had been hung upside down.

Very near him, at the entrance to the storehouse, looking out towards the fields, trees and sunshine, stood the farmer's wife, pounding barley with a huge wooden pestle. She looked tired and old. Her face was wrinkled, and was as brown as leather. Every now and then she stopped to wipe the perspiration that rolled down her face. As the badger watched her, a wicked plan formed in his mind.

"Dear lady," said the wily badger, "you must be very weary doing such heavy work in your old age. Won't you let me do that for you? My arms are very strong, and I could relieve you for a little while."

"Thank you for your kindness," said the old woman, "but I cannot let you do this work for me because I must not untie you, for you might escape if I did, and my husband would be very angry if he came home and found you gone."

Now, the badger is one of the most cunning of animals, and he said again in a very sad, gentle voice, "You are very unkind. You might untie me, for I promise not to try to escape. If you are afraid of your husband, I will let you bind me again before his return, when I have finished pounding the barley. I am so tired and sore tied up like this. If you would only let me down for just a few minutes I would indeed be very thankful!"

The old woman had a good and simple nature, and could not think badly of anyone. Much less did she think that the badger was only deceiving her in order to get away. She felt sorry, too, for the animal as she turned to look at him. The black-and-white, bristly creature looked in such a sad plight hanging downwards from the ceiling by his legs, which were all tied together tightly. So in the kindness of her heart, and believing the creature's promise that he would not run away, she untied the rope and let the badger down.

The old woman then gave him the big, heavy pestlc and told him to do the work for a short time while she rested. He took the solid piece of wood, but instead of doing the work as he was told, the badger at once sprang upon the old woman and knocked her down with it. He then killed her and made soup of her in her own kitchen. But even then the bad badger didn't escape to freedom. Oh no, he was more wicked than that. Instead he stayed and waited for the return of the old farmer.

The old man worked hard in his fields all day, and as he worked he thought with pleasure that no more now would his labour be spoiled by the destructive badger. Towards sunset he left his work and turned to go home. He was very tired, but the thought of the nice supper of hot badger soup awaiting his return cheered him. The thought that the badger might get free and take revenge on the poor old woman never once came into his mind.

He also never imagined that the badger knew magic. But of course, he did. And while the man was walking home, the badger used his dark arts to take on the old woman's shape. As soon as he saw the old farmer approaching he came out to greet him on the veranda of the little house, saying, "So you have come back at last. I have made the badger soup and have been waiting for you."

The old farmer quickly took off his straw sandals and sat

down before his tiny dinner-tray. The innocent man never even dreamed that it was not his wife but the badger who was waiting upon him, and asked at once for the soup.

Then the badger suddenly transformed himself back to his natural form and cried out, "You wife-eating old man!" Laughing loudly and scornfully he escaped out of the house and ran away to his den in the hills.

The old man was left behind alone. He was stunned into silence, and could hardly believe what he had seen and heard. As he realized what must have happened, and the whole truth sunk in, he was so scared and horrified that he fainted right away. After a while he came round and burst into tears. He cried loudly and bitterly. He rocked himself to and fro in his hopeless grief. It seemed too terrible to be real that his faithful old wife had been killed and cooked by the badger while he was working quietly in the fields, knowing nothing of what was going on at home, and congratulating himself on having once and for all got rid of the wicked animal who had so often spoiled his fields. And oh! The horrible thought – he had very nearly drunk the soup that the creature had made of his poor old wife.

"Oh dear, oh dear, oh dear!" he wailed aloud, clutching at himself and shaking his head in horror.

Now, not far away there lived in the same mountain a kind, good-natured old rabbit. He heard the old man crying and sobbing, and at once set out to see what was the matter, and if there was anything he could do to help his neighbour. The old man told him all that had happened. When the rabbit heard the story he was very angry at the wicked and deceitful badger, and told the old man to leave everything to him and he would avenge his wife's death. The farmer was at last comforted and, wiping away his tears, thanked the rabbit for his goodness in coming to him in his distress. The rabbit, seeing that the farmer was growing calmer, went back to his home to lay his plans for the punishment of the badger – for he was also very wise, as well as kind.

The next day the weather was fine, and the rabbit went out to find the badger. The evil creature was not to be seen in the woods or on the hillside or in the fields anywhere, so the rabbit went to his den and found the badger hiding there. Despite his dark magic powers, the animal had been afraid to show himself ever since he had escaped from the farmer's house, for fear of the old man's wrath.

The rabbit called out, "Why are you not out on such a beautiful day? Come out with me, and we will go and cut grass on the hills together."

The badger, never doubting that the gentle rabbit was his friend, willingly consented to go out with him, only too glad to get away from the neighbourhood of the farmer, and the fear of meeting him or being trapped once again.

The rabbit led the way miles from their homes, out on the hills where the grass grew tall and thick and sweet. They both set to work to cut down as much as they could carry home, to store it up for their winter's food. When they had each cut down all they wanted, they tied it in bundles and then started homewards, each carrying his bundle of grass on his back. This time the rabbit made the badger go first.

When they had gone a little way the rabbit took out a flint and steel, and, striking it over the badger's back as he stepped along in front, set his bundle of grass on fire. The badger heard the flint striking, and asked, "What is that noise, 'Crack, crack'?"

"Oh, that is nothing." replied the rabbit. "I only said 'Crack, crack' because this mountain is called Crackling Mountain."

The fire soon spread in the bundle of dry grass on the badger's back. Hearing the crackle of the

burning grass, the badger asked, "What is that?"

"Now we have come to the Burning Mountain," answered the rabbit.

By this time the bundle was nearly burned out and all the hair had been burned off the badger's back. He now knew what had happened by the smell of the smoke of the burning grass, and ran as fast as he could to his hole.

The rabbit followed and found him lying on his bed groaning with pain.

"What an unlucky fellow you are!" said the rabbit. "I can't imagine how this happened! I will bring you some medicine that will heal your back very quickly!"

The rabbit went away glad and smiling to think that the punishment upon the badger had already begun. He felt that nothing could be too bad for the animal who was guilty of murdering a poor, helpless old woman who had trusted him. He went home and made an ointment by mixing some sauce and red pepper together.

The rabbit carried this to the badger, but before putting it on he told him that it would cause him great pain, but that he must bear it patiently, because it was a wonderful medicine for burns and scalds and such wounds. The badger thanked him and begged him to apply it at once. No language can describe the pain of the badger as soon as the red pepper had been pasted all over his sore back. He rolled over and over and howled loudly. The rabbit, looking on, felt that the farmer's wife was beginning to be avenged.

The badger was in bed for about a month. But at last, in spite of the red pepper application, his burns healed and he got well. When the rabbit saw that the badger was getting well, he thought of another plan by which he could ensure the creature's death. So he went one day to pay the badger a visit and to congratulate him on his recovery. During the conversation the rabbit mentioned that he was going fishing, and described how pleasant fishing was when the weather was fine and the sea smooth.

The badger listened with pleasure to the rabbit's account of the way he passed his time now. He forgot all his pains and his month's illness, and thought what fun it would be if he could go fishing too. So he asked the rabbit if he would take him the next time he went out to fish. This was just what the rabbit wanted, so he agreed.

Then the rabbit went home and built two boats, one of wood and the other of clay. At last they were both finished, and as the rabbit stood and looked at his work he felt that all his trouble would be well rewarded if his plan succeeded, and he could manage to kill the wicked badger now.

The day came when the rabbit had arranged to take the badger fishing. He kept the wooden boat himself and gave the badger the clay one. The badger, who knew nothing about boats, was delighted with his new boat and thought how kind it was of the rabbit to give it to him.

They both got into their boats and set out. After going some distance from the shore the rabbit proposed that they should try their boats and see which one could go the quickest. The badger fell in with the proposal, and they both set to work to row as fast as they could for some time.

In the middle of the race the badger found his boat going to pieces, for the water now began to soften the clay. He cried out in great fear to the rabbit to help him. But the rabbit answered that he was avenging the old woman's murder, that this had been his intention all along, and that he was happy to think that the badger had at last met his deserts for all his evil crimes. Then he raised his oar and struck at the badger with all his strength till he fell with the sinking clay boat and was seen no more.

Thus at last he kept his promise to the old farmer. The rabbit now turned and rowed shorewards, and having landed and pulled his boat upon the beach, hurried back to tell the old farmer everything, and how the badger, his enemy, had been killed.

The old farmer thanked him with tears in his eyes. He said that till now he could never sleep at night or be at peace in the daytime, thinking of how his wife's death was unavenged, but from this time he would be able to sleep and eat as of old. He begged the rabbit to stay with him and share his home, so from this day the rabbit went to stay with the old farmer and they both lived together as good friends to the end of their days.

Beauty
and the
Beast

From *Europa's Fairy Tales* by Joseph Jacobs

There was once a merchant who had three daughters, and he loved them better than life itself. Now it happened that he had to travel on a long journey to buy some goods, and when he was just starting he said to them, "What shall I bring you back, my dears? Name any gift you like and it shall be yours."

The eldest daughter asked to have a necklace. The second daughter wished to have a gold chain. But the youngest daughter said, "Bring back yourself, Papa – that is what I want the most."

"Nonsense, child," said her father, "you must say something that I may remember to bring back for you. Surely there is something you wish for?"

"Then please bring me back a rose, Father," the youngest daughter answered.

Well, the merchant went on his journey and did his business in distant lands. He bought a pearl necklace for his eldest daughter, and a gold chain for his second daughter. But he knew it was no use getting a rose for the youngest while he was so far away, because it would fade and die before he got home. So he made up his mind he would get a rose for her the day he got near his house, so it stayed perfect for his beloved daughter.

When all his merchanting was done he rode off home and forgot all about finding a rose till he was almost home. Then he suddenly remembered what he had promised his youngest daughter, and looked about to see if he could find a beautiful bloom. Near where he had stopped he saw a great garden, and getting off his horse he wandered about in it till he found a lovely rose bush, and he plucked the most beautiful rose he could see on it. At that moment he heard a sudden crash like thunder, and looking around he saw a huge monster, with two tusks sticking out from its mouth, and fiery eyes surrounded by bristles, and horns coming out of its head and spreading over its back.

"Mortal," said the Beast, "who told you that you might pluck my roses?"

"Please, sir," said the merchant in fear and terror for his life. "I promised my daughter to bring her home a rose and forgot about it till the last moment. And then I saw your beautiful garden and thought you would not miss a single rose, or else I would have asked your permission."

"Thieving is thieving," said the Beast, "whether it be a rose or a diamond. Now you must pay with your life."

The merchant fell on his knees and begged for his life for the sake of his three daughters, who had none but him to work and support them.

"Well, mortal," said the Beast, "I grant your life on one condition – and one condition only. Seven days from now you must bring this youngest daughter of yours, for whose sake you have broken into my garden and committed this crime, and leave her here in your place. Otherwise, you must swear that you will return, and that you yourself will become my servant."

So the merchant made his promise by swearing solemnly and, taking his rose, mounted his horse. As he rode home, his heart was as heavy as lead, his mind full of woe.

As soon as he got into his house his daughters came rushing round him, clapping their hands and showing their joy in every way. The merchant tried hard not to show his anxiety and sorrow, and soon he gave the pearl necklace to his eldest daughter, and the gold chain to his second daughter. But when he gave the rose to his youngest, a deep sigh escaped his lips.

"Oh, thank you, Father," they all cried.

But the youngest said, "Why did you sigh so deeply when you gave me my rose?"

"Later on I will tell you," said the merchant, his eyes full of dread.

So for several days the family got on with everyday life as normal, though the merchant wandered about gloomy and sad, and nothing his daughters could do would cheer him up. At last he took his youngest daughter aside and said to her, "Bella, do you love your father?"

"Of course I do, Father, of course I do," the maiden replied.

"Well, now I have to ask that you do something because you love me – and it may well be the hardest thing that I ever have to ask of you," explained the merchant. And then he told her of all that had occurred with the Beast when he got the rose for her.

Bella was very upset, and then she said, "Oh, Father, it was all on account of me that you fell into the power of this Beast, so I will go with you to him.

Perhaps he will do me no harm, but even if he does, it is better that he does harm to me than evil to my dear father."

So next day the merchant took Bella behind him on his horse, as was the custom in those days, and they plodded off, hanging their heads, to the dwelling of the Beast. They allowed the horse to go as slowly as he liked, but the time finally came when they at last arrived.

The merchant and his daughter alighted from the horse to find that the doors of the house swung open on their own! And what do you think they saw there? Nothing! So they nervously went up the broad, stone steps and went through the great entrance hall, and into the grand dining room. There they saw a table spread with all manner of beautiful glasses and plates and dishes and cutlery, with plenty to eat upon it.

So they waited and they waited, thinking that the owner of the house would appear, till at last the merchant said, "Let's sit down and see what will happen then." And when they sat down invisible hands passed them things to eat and to drink, and they ate and drank to their heart's content. And when they arose from the table it arose too, and disappeared through the door as if it were being carried by invisible servants.

Suddenly there appeared before them the Beast, who said to the merchant, "Is this your youngest daughter?" And when the merchant told him that it was, the Beast said, "And is she willing to stop here with me?"

Then he looked at Bella who said, in a trembling voice, "Yes, sir."

"Well, no harm shall befall thee," replied the Beast, and Bella thought that she saw a kind light in his horrible eyes.

With that, he led the merchant down to his horse and told him he might come on the same day the following week to visit his daughter.

When the Beast returned to Bella, he said to her, "This house, with everything in it, is yours. If you want anything at all, just clap your hands and ask for it, and it will be brought to you." And with that he made a sort of bow and went away.

Bella lived on in the Beast's home of splendour and finery, and was waited on by invisible servants, and had whatever she liked to eat and to drink.

The next day, when the Beast came to her, though he looked so terrible, she had been so well treated that she had lost a great deal of her fear of him. So they spoke together about the gorgeous garden – which was quite the most beautiful she had ever seen or imagined – and about the house and about her father's business and about all manner of things, so that Bella lost altogether her dread of the Beast.

Before Bella knew it, a week had flown by, and her father came to see her. He found her quite happy, and he felt much less worry of her fate at the hands of the Beast. So it went on for many days, Bella seeing and talking to the Beast every day, till she got to quite like him.

One day the Beast did not come at his usual time, and Bella missed him awfully. She searched all over the house, but could find no sign of him at all. So she wandered about the garden trying to find him, calling out his name, but received no reply. Bella's heart began to race with anxiety. Then at last she came to the rose bush from which her father had plucked the rose, and there, under it, was the Beast lying, huddled up, without any life or motion. She threw herself down by his side, dreadfully shocked and upset, remembering all the kindness that the Beast had shown her. She began to sob, saying, "Oh, Beast, Beast, why did you die? I was getting to love you so much."

No sooner had she uttered these words than the hide of the Beast split in two and out came the most handsome young prince! He told her that he had been enchanted by a magician and that he could not recover his natural form unless a maiden should, of her own accord, declare that she loved him.

Thereupon the prince sent for the merchant and his daughters, and he was married to Bella, and they all lived happily ever after.

The Goblin Pony

From Andrew Lang's *Grey Fairy Book*

There was once an old woman named Peggy, whose daughter and husband had died, leaving her to look after her three grandchildren alone. The eldest was a boy who was of the age to want to be out and about by himself, having an eye for the girls. The next grandchild was a daughter, who was kind and hard-working, and helped Peggy to look after the family. The youngest grandchild was a little boy called Richard, of whom Peggy was especially fond.

One particularly cold, dark night, Peggy felt a

chill of fear spread through her old bones, and she gave her grandchildren a solemn warning. "Don't stir from the fireplace tonight," she said, "for the wind is blowing so violently that the house shakes. Besides, this is Halloween, when the witches are abroad and the goblins, who are their servants, are wandering about in all sorts of disguises, doing harm to the children of men."

"Why should I stay here?" said the eldest of the young people. "No, I must go and see what the daughter of old Jacob, the rope-maker, is doing. She wouldn't close her blue eyes all night if I didn't visit her father before the moon had gone down."

"I must go and catch lobsters and crabs," said the granddaughter. "If I don't, I will have nothing to sell at market tomorrow and we will stay hungry at supper time! Not all the witches and goblins in the world shall hinder me from going out tonight."

So they all determined to go on their business or pleasure, and scorned the wise advice of old Peggy. Only the youngest child hesitated a minute, when she said to him, "You stay here, my little Richard, and I will tell you beautiful stories." But he wanted to pick a bunch of wild thyme and some blackberries by moonlight, and ran out after the others.

When they got outside they said, "The old woman talks of wind and storm, but never was the weather finer or the sky more clear!"

Then all of a sudden they noticed a little pony close beside them, which not one of them had heard approach.

"Oh, ho!" they said. "That must be old Farmer Valentine's new pony. Perhaps it has escaped from its stable

and is going down to drink at the pond."

"My pretty little pony," said the eldest, patting the creature, "you mustn't run too far. I'll take you to the pond myself."

With these words he jumped on the pony's back. He was quickly followed by his sister, who reached down a hand and helped little Richard swing himself astride, for he didn't like to be left behind.

Off they set to the pond, trotting along in the moonlight. On the way, they met several of their companions, and they invited them all to mount the pony, which they did, and the little creature did not seem to mind the extra weight, but jogged merrily on.

The quicker it trotted the more the young people enjoyed the fun. They dug their heels into the pony's sides and called out, "Gallop, little pony, you have never had such brave riders before!"

In the meantime the wind had risen again, and the waves began to howl. But the pony did not seem to mind the noise, and instead of going to the pond, cantered gaily towards the seashore.

Richard began to regret not going to gather his thyme and blackberries, and the eldest brother seized the pony by the mane and tried to make it turn round, for he remembered the blue eyes of Jacob the rope-maker's daughter. But he tugged and pulled in vain, for the pony galloped straight on into the sea, till the waves met its forefeet. As soon as it felt the water it neighed and capered about with glee, advancing quickly into the foaming billows. When the waves had covered the children's legs they repented their careless behaviour, and

cried out, "The cursed little pony is bewitched. If we had only listened to old Peggy's advice we shouldn't have been lost."

The further the pony advanced, the higher rose the sea. At last the waves covered the children's heads and they were all drowned.

Towards morning old Peggy went out, for she was anxious about the fate of her grandchildren. But she could not find them anywhere. She asked all the neighbours if they had seen the children, but no one knew anything about them, except that the eldest had not been with the blue-eyed daughter of Jacob the rope-maker. Indeed, several of them were searching for their own missing girls and boys.

As Peggy was going home, bowed with grief, she saw a little pony coming towards her. When it got quite near her it neighed loudly, and galloped past her so quickly that in a moment it was out of sight.

The Jelly Fish and the Monkey

From *Japanese Fairy Tales* by Yei Theodora Ozaki

Long ago, in old Japan, in the days when the jelly fish was a hard creature with a shell and bones, the oceans were governed by Rin Jin, the Dragon King of the Sea. He was the ruler of all sea creatures both great and small, and lived in a palace at the bottom of the ocean so beautiful that no one has ever seen anything like it, even in dreams. But despite all this, the Dragon King was not happy, for he reigned on his own and was lonely. Finally he decided to find a wife and called several fish ambassadors to search the oceans for a suitable bride.

At length they brought to the palace a lovely young dragon, with scales like the glittering green of the waves and eyes the gleaming white of pearls, whom the King fell in love with at once. The wedding was celebrated with great splendour and every living thing in the oceans rejoiced, from the hugest whale to the tiniest shrimp.

The Dragon King and his bride were very happy together – but for just two months, for then the Dragon Queen suddenly fell very ill. The desperate King ordered the best doctor and nurses to look after her, but instead of getting better, the young Queen grew gradually worse. The doctor tried to excuse himself by saying that although he knew the right kind of medicine, it was impossible to find it in the sea.

"Please tell me what it is!" demanded the Dragon King.

"The liver cut from a live monkey!" answered the doctor. "If we could only get that, Her Majesty would soon recover."

"Well, even though we sea creatures cannot leave the ocean, we must get a monkey to cut up somehow," decided the King.

He called his chief steward for advice, who thought for some time, and declared, "I know! The jelly fish is ugly to look at, but he has a hard shell and four bony legs and can walk on land. An island where there are monkeys lies a few hours' swim to the south – let us send the jelly fish there. If he can't catch a monkey, maybe he can trick one into coming here."

The jelly fish was summoned and ordered to entice a monkey to the Dragon King's palace. Although very worried about the task, the poor jelly fish had no choice but to swim off at once.

Luckily, when he reached Monkey Island he saw a big pine tree and on one of its branches was just what he was looking for – a live monkey.

"How do you do, Mr Monkey?" called the jelly fish, thinking quickly of a plan. "Isn't it a lovely day?" he added politely.

"A very fine day," answered the monkey. "I have never seen you before. What is your name?"

"My name is Jelly Fish. I have heard so much of your beautiful island that I have come to see it."

"I am very glad to see you," said the monkey.

"By the by," said the jelly fish, "have you seen the palace of the Dragon King of the Sea where I live?"

"I have often heard of it, but I have never seen it!" answered the monkey.

"Then you ought most surely to come. The beauty of the palace is beyond all description – it is certainly the most lovely place in the world," said the jelly fish, and he described the beauty and grandeur of the Sea King's palace.

The monkey grew more and more interested, and came down the tree. "I should love to come with you," he sighed, "but I can't swim."

"There is no difficulty about that. I can carry you on my back," said the jelly fish.

So the excited monkey leaped onto the jelly fish's hard shell and the creature plunged into the sea.

Thus they went along, skimming through the waves until they were about halfway, when the jelly fish began to feel more and more sorry for the terrible fate that lay ahead for the monkey. With a sigh, he told the monkey everything – how he was to be killed for his liver, to save the Dragon Queen.

The poor monkey was horrified, and very angry at the trick played upon him. But he was clever, so tried to keep calm and think of some way to escape.

A bright thought struck him, and he said quite cheerfully, "What a pity it was, Mr Jelly Fish, that you did not tell me before we left the island! I have several livers and would happily have given you one – but I have left them all hanging on the pine tree."

The jelly fish was very disappointed, for he believed the story.

"Never mind," said the monkey, "take me back to where you found me and I will fetch a liver."

The pleased jelly fish turned his course towards Monkey Island once more. But no sooner had he reached the shore than the sly monkey scampered up into the pine tree and jeered at him. "Of course, I won't give you my liver, but come and get it if you can!" mocked the monkey.

There was nothing for the jelly fish to do but return to the Dragon King and confess his failure.

Of course, the Dragon King was beside himself

with fury. He ordered a terrible punishment – that all the bones were to be drawn out from the jelly fish's body, that he was to be beaten until his shell broke off, and then banished from the palace.

The jelly fish, humiliated and horrified beyond all words, cried out for pardon. But the Dragon King's order had to be obeyed. And that is why the descendents of the jelly fish have all been soft and boneless, just as you see them today, thrown up by the waves high upon the shores of Japan.

The Strange Visitor

From Joseph Jacobs' *English Fairy Tales*

A woman was sitting at her reel one night.

And still she sat, and still she reeled, and still she wished for company.

In came a pair of broad broad feet, and sat down at the fireside.

And still she sat, and still she reeled, and still she wished for company.

In came a pair of small small legs, and sat down on the broad broad feet.

And still she sat, and still she reeled, and still she

wished for company.

In came a pair of thick thick knees, and sat down on the small small legs.

And still she sat, and still she reeled, and still she wished for company.

In came a pair of thin thin thighs, and sat down on the thick thick knees.

And still she sat, and still she reeled, and still she wished for company.

In came a pair of huge huge hips, and sat down on the thin thin thighs.

And still she sat, and still she reeled, and still she wished for company.

In came a wee wee waist, and sat down on the huge huge hips.

And still she sat, and still she reeled, and still she wished for company.

In came a pair of broad broad shoulders, and sat down on the wee wee waist.

And still she sat, and still she reeled, and still she wished for company.

In came a pair of small small arms, and sat down on the broad broad shoulders.

And still she sat, and still she reeled, and still she wished for company.

In came a pair of huge huge hands, and sat down on the small small arms.

And still she sat, and still she reeled, and still she wished for company.

In came a small small neck, and sat down on the broad broad shoulders.

And still she sat, and still she reeled, and still she wished for company.

In came a huge huge head, and sat down on the small small neck.

"How did you get such broad broad feet?" said the woman.

"Much tramping, much tramping." (*gruffly*)

"How did you get such small small legs?"

"Aih-h-h!–late–and wee-e-e–moul." (*whiningly*)

"How did you get such thick thick knees?"

"Much praying, much praying." (*piously*)

"How did you get such thin thin thighs?"

"Aih-h-h!–late–and wee-e-e–moul." (*whiningly*)

"How did you get such huge huge hips?"

"Much sitting, much sitting." (*gruffly*)

"How did you get such a wee wee waist?"

"Aih-h-h!–late–and wee-e-e–moul." (*whiningly*)

"How did you get such broad broad shoulders?"

"With carrying broom, with carrying broom." (*gruffly*)

"How did you get such small small arms?"

"Aih-h-h!–late–and wee-e-e–moul." (*whiningly*)

"How did you get such huge huge hands?"

"Threshing with an iron flail, threshing with an iron flail." (*gruffly*)

"How did you get such a small small neck?"

"Aih-h-h!–late–wee-e-e–moul." (*pitifully*)

"How did you get such a huge huge head?"

"Much knowledge, much knowledge." (*keenly*)

"What do you come for?"

(*At the top of the voice, with a wave of the arm and a stamp of the feet.*) "FOR YOU!"

The End